BUZZ CLUB

Also by Xena Knox

Sh!t Bag

XENA KNOX
BUZZ CLUB

Content warning: contains sexual references and coercive behaviour.

HODDER CHILDREN'S BOOKS

First published in Great Britain in 2025 by Hodder & Stoughton Limited

1 3 5 7 9 10 8 6 4 2

Text copyright © 2025 Xena Knox Limited

Xena Knox has asserted her right to be identified as the author of this work.

All characters and events in this publication, other than those clearly in the public domain, are fictitious and any resemblance to real persons, living or dead, is purely coincidental.

All rights reserved.

No part of this publication may be reproduced, stored in a retrieval system, or transmitted, in any form or by any means, without the prior permission in writing of the publisher, nor be otherwise circulated in any form of binding or cover other than that in which it is published and without a similar condition including this condition being imposed on the subsequent purchaser.

A CIP catalogue record for this book is available from the British Library.

ISBN 978 1 444 97208 5

Typeset in Goudy Old Style BT by Palimpsest Book Production Ltd, Falkirk, Stirlingshire
Printed and bound in Great Britain by Clays Ltd, Elcograf S.p.A.

The paper and board used in this book are made from wood from responsible sources.

Hodder Children's Books
An imprint of
Hachette Children's Group
Part of Hodder & Stoughton Limited
Carmelite House
50 Victoria Embankment
London EC4Y 0DZ

The authorised representative in the EEA is Hachette Ireland, 8 Castlecourt Centre, Dublin 15, D15 XTP3, Ireland (email: info@hbgi.ie)

An Hachette UK Company
www.hachette.co.uk

www.hachettechildrens.co.uk

Praise for *Sh!t Bag*

'Funny, direct, real-feeling and romantic, this superb
YA debut conveys the reality of managing life
with an ostomy'
Guardian

'What could have been another "issues" book is elevated
by Knox's writing and her whip-smart and honest main
character. A funny and charming read'
Irish Independent

'A compelling and insightful read that sheds a
brilliant light on hugely important topics'
Glamour

'This bold, brilliantly funny book is the best YA novel
I've read this year. Xena Knox is one to watch!'
Cat Clarke, author of *Girlhood*

'A must read! With disability representation and
written from Xena's own experience, it's full of sass,
humour, embarrassing moments and something all
teens will love. Xena's characters feel SO real,
you'll be hooked from the first page'
A. M. Dassu, author of *Boy, Everywhere*

'What an incredible read! Freya is feisty & unfiltered – and now she has an ileostomy bag & is furious. This unflinching story of disgust, humiliation and hard-won wins educated me in the most entertaining of ways . . . Highly recommend'
Sue Wallman, author of *Lying About Last Summer*

'A sharp, funny book that addresses a hidden issue'
The School Librarian

TO MY SUPER HERO.

CHAPTER 1

TAVI

Axel shrugs. 'I just think we need different things from the relationship, Tavi.'

'Sex—!' I snap.

He flinches like we're not alone in the bus shelter and I'm publicly embarrassing the both of us. 'Now you're being aggressive,' he says.

'I'm not being aggressive,' I say quieter. 'I'm pointing out we need different things from . . . the sex.'

Axel looks away down the street and says, 'Yeah, well . . .'

Is that all I'm worth? *Yeah, well.* After everything I've done. Everything I've let him do. All he leaves me with is a *yeah, well?*

'Maybe best I don't come to your birthday thing on Sunday . . .' he says, kicking his heel against a paving stone. 'It'll be too—'

'You have a whitehead! On the side of your nose.'

He flicks open his phone and uses it like a mirror. 'How long's that been there?' he asks.

I shrug. 'Lunch . . . ?' I've only just noticed it. But let him think he had a pus-filled zit on his picture-perfect face, all the way through double Spanish, when he was snuggled up beside Larissa Perfect Fucking Hair Ferucci.

I flare my nostrils as he scratches off the offending spot. 'It's bleeding now,' I say helpfully.

'Yes!' he says exasperated.

'Maybe put hand sanitiser on it, so it doesn't get infected.'

He glances at me quickly. 'Do you have any?'

'No . . .' I say dripping derision, knowing there's a bottle in my bag. 'Larissa will.'

Axel blinks.

Those long eyelashes . . . I hate myself.

He prods his index finger against the bleeding area and says, 'This is supposed to be fun – relationships . . .'

I can't stop my snort. 'Fun? Not with us it's not.' I fold my arms across my front defensively and chew on my thumbnail. All I can think about is touching his cheek now. *My face touching his cheek.* I should give him the sanitiser.

'You want me to say sorry?'

I don't reply. And stare just past him, at the dusty grime collected in the gap between the shelter's glass wall and its metal frame. Numbly, I say, 'You're right. We need different things from a *relationship*.' A vehicle looms into my window's view, and I realise it's Axel's bus. He shifts – he's seen it too.

I look down at my balled, soggy tissue and sniff.

'I have to go,' Axel says.

I stare at the empty tarmac where the bus used to be and struggle to swallow the lump in my throat – just like Tuesday night when Axel grabbed me there and called me a slut.

CHAPTER 2

LISS

Ella chucks her phone on her desk and returns her focus to her iMac, and the YouTube girl tapping a frozen mini doughnut on a table. 'Axel's finally dumped Tavi,' she says, sliding the video forward.

'Oh no! Poor Tavi,' I say, setting my Diet Coke on Ella's bedside table and standing. 'Do you need to go see her?'

'Nah. She'll be all neg.'

'You sure?' I say, hovering. 'Was that her?'

'Maz. He's with Axel now. They've gone for burgers.'

I wait for Ella to expand on why that means she's not calling Tavi to check in on her. But Ella seems engrossed with the ASMR video.

I sit again.

'As much as I hate that arrogant prick,' Ella adds, 'you

can't totally blame him. Axel told Maz she refuses to put out now.'

'Oh . . .' I say, as if that explains everything. I bite my lip so I don't say what I really think.

'I mean, it's not like she's a virgin!' Ella says. 'They were shagging before, weren't they.'

'Um, I don't know . . .'

Ella clicks through to another ASMR-mukbang creator and falls silent.

I check the time. I need to get going.

Ella suddenly swings round in her chair to glare at me, and says, 'If Maz even *dared* to dump me, never mind go for burgers after!'

Frozen like that mini doughnut, I manage, 'He wouldn't dare.'

'No. He knows I'd cut his balls off!'

I nod. Because what do you say to that?

'Anyway,' Ella says, swinging back to her iMac. 'I should probably make an effort and give Tavi something for her birthday. Want to come in on it with me?'

'Me?'

'Yeah.'

'If you think . . . I don't have much money.'

Ella grunts and waves a hand dismissively. 'There'll be something in Mum's promo cupboard.' And mutters, 'She's never free. Never initiates messaging. Not since Mr

I-Carry-A-Nail-File-In-My-Pencil-Case got in her knickers— Want to get a burger? I need a Bloat Burger now I know the boys are there.'

'I should get home,' I say carefully, then admit, 'I've got running club tonight.'

'Course you do,' Ella says, baring her teeth. 'Right, well, eff off then.' She shoos me.

I stand and fix the cushion I've crushed on the chair. Take my Diet Coke can, to put in the kitchen recycling.

Ella's flicking through her phone. She looks up at me. 'You still here?'

'No, I'm going.'

'Good.' But she gets up and walks out ahead of me. I follow her downstairs, presuming she's seeing me out. Until she stops by the big carved wardrobe at the door and strains up on tiptoe to look inside.

'I'll just get rid of my can . . . ?' I say.

'And?' Ella replies from inside the cupboard.

I'm washing the Coke's stickiness from my fingers, when I hear a scream out in the hall. 'You okay—?' I shout. But when I get to Ella, I find she's doubled over laughing.

She points at me and says, 'You're definitely coming with me to Tavi's birthday on Sunday!'

CHAPTER 3

TAVI

'Happy birthday!'

I look over Ella's shoulder and lock eyes with Larissa – who's standing in *my* hallway, on *my* birthday, wishing me a *happy birthday*.

'Larissa,' I say coldly, letting go of Ella to glare ice at her too. 'This is your idea of *a fun, girly afternoon* is it, Ella?'

Ella wiggles a finger at me and grins. 'That's still to come!'

Mum sticks her head out from the family room. 'We've not quite finished setting up— Oh, hello!' She practically skips down the hall and beams at Larissa. 'Now, who are you again?'

'Larissa Ferucci. I'm in Tavi's year.'

'Larissa . . . ?' Mum frowns. 'Have we met?'

'No, Mum,' I say sharply. Please shut up. You definitely *do not* recognise her.

I can see Mum admiring Larissa's long, blonde, bouncy hair and – as I dreaded – gives an almost imperceptible nod of recognition, smirks, purses her lips like she's fighting hysterics, then says, 'Why don't you girlies pop upstairs? I'll shout when we're set.'

I have no desire to *pop* anywhere with Larissa, thanks, never mind up to my room! But the fact Mum's now laughing at me – I can't handle further humiliation if she says something. So, I lead the way upstairs.

A few weeks back, Mum interrupted me mid-creation of a *new* hair and make-up style. She'd immediately laughed that although I looked *lovely*, I didn't really look *myself*. It wasn't till she left me alone that I remembered my iPad was propped up beside me, open on Larissa's Instagram, zoomed in on a picture of her from Axel's birthday party the week before. With the exact same big, bouncy blowout I was attempting to recreate.

That was the birthday party that Axel told Larissa – in front of everyone – that she looked *fire*.

So . . . well, you probably get where I'm going with this. Sad, pathetic little old me thought I'd try and see if I could light a paltry match in my boyfriend's boxers by making myself look as luscious and bouncy as his ex-girlfriend. Larissa Perfect Fucking Hair Ferucci.

Lot of good that did me!

* * *

Up in my room, Ella drops onto my bed, unzips her rucksack and pulls out a birthday card and folded, pink gift bag. 'This is the best thing I've ever given anyone! Shut the door, Liss!' she demands.

Larissa shuts my door.

'Not being rude, Larissa,' I say, trying to block her view of my photo wall filled with pictures of me and Axel, 'but why are you here?'

Larissa glances to Ella. 'Ella said . . .'

Ella interjects, 'You're not exactly heavy in the friends department these days, Tavi. Especially now Axel—'

Fully aware of my shit life, I cut Ella off. 'Who'd need enemies with friends like Larissa—?' I turn my glare on Larissa to make it clear she doesn't intimidate me.

Larissa blinks like one of those innocent baby dolls with long eyelashes. And says like she's confused, 'Umm, what have *I* done?'

'You know!' I snap. She wants to humiliate me. Especially now Axel's dumped me.

Larissa looks to Ella for help.

'You got any popcorn?' Ella says, leaning back ready for the show.

I death-glare Ella and turn on Larissa again. 'You called me a cock-tease. What else? Oh yeah, a skank. Cheap! Messy . . . Apparently I smell like own-brand washing powder! My hair's greasy. I have blackheads the size of potholes—'

Ella blurts, 'What the hell, Tavi?'

My heart's thundering I'm so pumped with adrenaline. Reliving the shame I felt the first time I heard these things Larissa said about me. How I've had them spinning round and round in my head ever since. How I've felt worthless and low. A nobody.

Watched the way Axel lights up when he's around her, despite everything she's said about me. Their history, together. I can't look at Larissa anymore. I'm all out of bravery. I do, however, look at Ella.

Her mouth is gaping and she's flushed, frowning at Larissa. She says, 'You never said that . . . ! Did you?'

Larissa whispers, 'Of course not. Never.'

I say, 'Axel said you'd deny it!'

ELLA

The doorbell rings downstairs.

'Did you invite anyone else?' Tavi snaps.

Jeez, nippy much! 'No,' I say.

She rushes out onto the landing and shouts down, 'I'll get the door!'

I toss Tavi's gift out of the way and go to the landing myself, to lean over the banister. If Axel just slimes his way back in again . . . ! I watch Tavi downstairs, she flips her hair to add volume. Pauses, and opens the front door. And with a bang, confetti and rainbow tissue-shards cannon into her hall, blocking her from view. A chorus of *Happy Birthdays* and bodies and foil balloons crowd inside and move along the hall out of sight. Tavi closes the front door and stares along the corridor as I hear *hellos* further inside. I can definitely hear a male voice . . . Is it him? It would be typical of Axel to rock up and act like nothing's changed.

Tavi's stock-still, back against her front door.

'Who is it?' I hiss over the banister.

She glances up at me, says apathetically, 'My sister's mate. Her mum. And my mum's best friend. Happy Birthday to me!' Then snaps suddenly into aggy mode, 'Why would you bring Larissa—?'

I sigh and reach back to pull Tavi's bedroom door shut so Liss can't hear us, but Tavi must think I'm blanking her because she runs up the stairs.

'Chill out,' I whisper, holding up my hand. 'I was shutting the door.'

'Why did you bring her? Do you love humiliating me that much?'

'No one's trying to humiliate you, Tavi. Not me or Liss anyway. I actually thought you'd get on. We'd have a laugh.'

'Great idea. Let's laugh about how Liss is perfect and . . . I'm *such a skank* that Axel can't get it up anymore and that's why he's dumped me because he finds me repellent compared with Larissa Fucking Perfect Hair Ferucci!'

I frown, running Tavi's words over in my head again.

Tavi blinks furiously and wipes away her angry tears.

I hadn't quite realised that Axel's succeeded in completely obliterating Tavi's self-confidence.

Tavi's eyes flash to her bedroom door. 'That was a joke about Axel not being able to . . . I'm just . . .'

'Course it was . . .' I say carefully.

She nods, and just stands there looking tired. Finally she says, 'Seeing as it's my birthday, do you think you and Larissa could maybe come down and try and make things a little bit fun for me?' And she walks back downstairs.

CHAPTER 4

TAVI

'Presents time, everyone!' Mum calls an hour in, appearing from the hallway lugging an iceberg-shaped birthday present.

'Ooh, presents!' Milly's best mate, Anusha, giggles uncontrollably.

I wasn't going to share our smuggled Prosecco with my sister and her pal, especially after Anusha kept asking where Axel is – least Ella and Larissa didn't say anything when I told her he was at his granny's – but then Milly caught us swigging it on the patio and threatened to tell Mum if we didn't share. Now Anusha's laughing at anything and everything and Milly has the hiccups.

'We're doing retro pass-the-parcel,' Mum says. 'Come on, everyone! Sit round in a circle.'

Milly and Anusha collapse obediently onto the rug and

squeal when Douglas our pug jumps up, trying to lick their faces.

'Mum,' I hiss. 'We're not playing games!' What happened to the *chill birthday afternoon* she promised?

She death-stares me to shut up. I glare back, but as her eyes slide to her best friend, Ally, I get the impression this wasn't so much Mum's idea.

'Dave!' Ally pipes up. 'You too. Come join. Bring more Prosecco with you!'

Dad's eating leftover tacos in the kitchen but good-naturedly manages to find a bottle and joins us. Strangely, seeing Dad folded self-consciously into a gap in the circle makes me feel almost okay that my birthday's been invaded by my mum's and sister's friends. The last time we played pass-the-parcel with both my parents, I was eight. I smile at Dad and he smiles back.

Ella nudges my knee and mouths, *'Pass-the-parcel? Really?'*

I shrug and focus away from her, onto Mum. It's still my birthday and Ella being neg really isn't helping.

'Usual rules,' Mum says. 'Music plays, we pass the parcel. Music stops, you peel off a layer of wrapping. And inside each, there's a gift for Tavi. And a *present* for everyone else—'

Anusha claps excitedly.

'Or!' Ally interrupts. 'There's a task and forfeit! You might regret holding the parcel when the music stops!'

Anusha gasps. Milly hiccups. Ella sighs beside me.

'Ready?' Mum says, already filming us.

'Ready!' Ally says.

Mum strikes play on the music. 'Pass the parcel!'

I shove it to Anusha, who, bouncing along to the music, rolls it on to Milly, who passes it to Anusha's mum, then Dad. Ally is next, and Mum stops the music. Mum catcalls as Ally rips the turquoise and silver-starred paper.

Inside are inflatable pink-flamingo can holders for each of us. Everyone blows theirs up except for Ella, who leaves hers flat beside our feet. Why can't she just join in for once? Axel would've joined in. He loved family games night . . . A slim, pale-pink present and card are handed to me. I open them to find a contour-and-eyeshadow palette from Anusha and her mum.

I thank them, the paper's shoved out of the circle for Douglas to maul, and the music starts again.

Next, the music stops on Milly. 'This iz my prE-Zent,' she hiccups, pushing the revealed silver envelope across the circle.

But before I can even slide my thumb below the flap, Mum snaps, 'Ah! Wait, this time there's a task!'

Ally finds a sheet of notepaper among the discarded wrapping and reads it out, 'Describe Tavi's gift to her without naming it. If she can't guess what it is then your forfeit is to do an impression of a gorilla with hiccups.'

Milly goes straight to her impression. 'OOo OOo ICK!'

'Tavi's meant to guess first,' Ella drawls. 'I vote little sis does a task that isn't channelling her spirit animal.'

Milly scrunches her nose at Ella. 'Jeal-ous muCH?'

'Jealous you make a convincing drunk chimp? I don't think so.'

'Gor-illA!'

I eye Mum and Dad. Milly needs to be more subtle. I'm dead if they realise her hiccups are because I gave her Prosecco and not mocktails. 'Maybe I should just open it?' I say, tearing the envelope quickly to discover that Milly's bought us family tickets to Dundee's Anime and Comic Con, DeeCon. 'Awesome, Milly, thanks!'

'You didn't let her describe it!' Ella shouts. 'Forfeit!'

I'm starting to wish I could forfeit Ella right now.

'Gorilla with hiccups it is!' Mum says. 'Tavi, you have to do it.'

I'm tempted to object, but instead I say half-heartedly, 'Ooo, Oo, Oo hick-up . . . ?'

Ella taps her forefinger on her chin and says, 'Little sis's was more realistic!'

All the mums are filming now. 'Pass the parcel!' Mum calls, pressing play again on the music and slapping her thigh in time to the beat. 'Round and round it goes!' she hollers. 'Where will it stop? Nobody knows!'

'Woo-hoo!' Anusha's mum yelps, chucking the parcel to Dad. Who chucks it to Ally just as the music stops.

Ally kicks it back to Dad. 'You go, Dave,' she says, as she, Anusha's mum and my mum train their phones on him.

Dad glances to me for permission, grinning. I nod encouragingly. He's fingers and thumbs as he carefully tears the purple layer away to reveal—

'Fuck!' Ella says.

We all snap to look at her.

'Keep the language clean, girls!' Mum warns. The other mums agree.

Then Larissa says, 'Oh my God!'

I glance to Larissa and back to Ella, and to where they're both staring – at Dad.

He waves a folded pink gift bag at me. 'Who's this one from?' he says looking around the circle. Douglas bounces into the circle, trying to get his teeth on the present.

'That was upstairs!' Ella says incredulous.

'We've put all the gifts inside *the parcel*,' Mum explains. 'Hurry and open it. Ours is next. Douglas, go to your bed!'

Dad reads the slip of paper with the task. 'Each guest must take a turn—'

'I don't feel so good!' Larissa blurts.

Dad glances at Larissa, unsure whether to proceed.

Mum says, 'Larissa, do you want to go to the bathroom . . . ? Or into the garden for some fresh air?'

'Yes—!' Larissa bolts out to the hall. We hear her thunder upstairs and the bathroom door slam shut.

'Do you think it was those gloopy pink drinks?' Anusha's mum muses.

Mum turns on her. 'Excuse me! My Tavi Tornado mocktails were not *gloopy*, they're packed full of superfoods!'

'Should I continue . . . ?' Dad says unsure. Mum waves her hand to get a move on. So Dad reads brightly, 'The birthday girl must describe her next gift through mime—'

Ella's in the middle of downing one of the mums' Proseccos when Dad says this and suddenly chokes so badly that she's ushered outside to sit on the garden bench with a glass of water.

'Maybe we should pause for a bit,' Dad says to Mum, coming back inside. 'We can finish opening the presents later when they've calmed down.'

'No!' Mum growls. 'Our present's in the middle layer!' She grabs the pink gift bag from the sofa and shoves it into my hands. 'Mime it. Then it's our present.'

ELLA

Once they've returned to the living room, I'm straight on the phone to Liss. 'Where are you?'

'Upstairs.'

'No shit! Where upstairs?'

'Locked in the bathroom.'

'Can you climb out the window?'

'What? Where are you?'

'In the garden.'

'Why—? Have they opened it?'

'Not yet. Actually . . .' I move to the back wall of Tavi's house and peer round the frame of the patio door. 'Aww, shit. She's got the case out of the bag.'

'Who?'

'Tavi. Uh . . . she's turned away from them all at least. Maybe she won't say . . . !'

'What was the task? What does she have to do?'

'Thank fuck I talked you into coming here with me. No one'll believe this played out like it has without a witness.'

'The mums are live-streaming it, Ella!'

'No need to shout!'

'I'm not shouting. I just don't think you realise how bad this is!'

'You're right . . .' I hang up on Liss. Flick to camera and start filming.

TAVI

Inside the neoprene case, behind a protective plastic window, is a purple, pebble shaped, rubbery item. With a folded USB cable, a silky pouch and some little square packets . . . I slide my finger below the plastic casing and touch the silicone surface of the thing inside – it's firm. So not a squishy stress ball then . . . ? It looks a bit like—

'Hurry up,' Mum says.

'I don't know what it is . . . !' I say.

'I'll have a go!' Anusha pipes up in her usual perky princess fashion. She joins me by the monstera plant, takes the case and peers in through the protective window, and gives it a sniff. She whispers, 'Is it an electric razor? Smells soapy like lavender.'

'There's no blade . . .' I murmur back.

'Maybe one of those things that pluck the hairs out or zaps them?'

Milly appears beside us and hiccup-glances back towards the open door to the hall. I follow her eyes. Larissa's on the stairs making a cutting gesture across her neck with her hand. I raise my eyebrows at Milly questioningly. She shrugs. I glance to the garden to see Ella at the window, filming me. She grins, gives me a thumbs up and flicks her hand as if to hurry me along with her present.

'BzzzZZZZ!' Anusha turns to the parents still holding my gift in its case and buzzes like an angry bee, running it up her leg wincing and jerking like she's experiencing intermittent electric shocks from a hidden hair zapper. 'Oww, ohh! Bzzzzz!'

The mums stare at Anusha. Dad stares at Anusha. Ella's

now inside and standing behind the kitchen island staring at Anusha, her mouth gaping.

I glance back to Larissa. She's at the door now, looking panicked. She points to Anusha, signals across her throat again and then performs a graphic hand gesture that makes me look quickly to the mums and Dad to check they haven't seen her.

Anusha's now running her imaginary hair-plucking torture device under her armpit and onwards up onto her face, across her top lip, 'Bzzzzz! Ohh! Oaww!' and along her chin.

The adults are frozen, stunned. Ella's quivering in silent hysterics, holding her mobile high. And Larissa? Larissa has turned beetroot, gripping the door frame, desperately clutching her neck and shaking her head.

Anusha notices her just after me, stops her buzzing and bellows, 'What's wrong with Larissa? She's choking! Quick – Larissa's got something stuck in her throat!'

Larissa freezes. Releases her neck. Then, as if she's just realised she does indeed have something stuck there, grabs it again. She nods. Staggers into the living area, making a sound like you do when your mouth is full of toothpaste but don't know where to spit it out. The parents leap into action and run to her. Anusha and Milly scramble over the sofa after them. Douglas barks. And Mum wallops Larissa on the back.

Larissa squeals, 'EOW!'

'Oh sorry, love! Are you okay?'

Larissa coughs. Unnaturally. Flaps her arm. Points. Mum slaps her on the back again.

'EOW!'

'Larissa, love – are you actually choking?'

Larissa flaps her arm again and points to the floor. I look to where she's pointing, to the weird gift strewn in bits across the rug where Anusha's chucked it in the panic.

The gift . . .

The gift that Ella and Larissa planned on giving me upstairs . . . In private!

'Try the Heimlich!' Anusha says, circling.

'Stop!' I shout.

Everyone swings to look at me.

'I mean, we should stop – take a break. From opening presents?'

Larissa nods furiously.

'Yeah. We should . . . ?' I'm stumped, haven't a clue what Larissa wants us to do.

'Go upstairs and have a lie-down . . .' Larissa prompts, crystal clear despite her recent asphyxiation. 'We'll just clear all this mess away first— Help tidy up.' And she flits across the rug, scooping up the scattered pieces of her and Ella's gift and runs out into the hall and up the stairs again.

'But there's still our present!' Mum wails.

Dad says to me, 'Is the blonde girl okay?'

'She's fine,' I say.

I catch Ella out of the corner of my eye, moving round the sofa to get a good angle, so she can get us all in on camera.

'Bring her back to open the last present then!' Mum says.

'Leave it,' Dad says to Mum. 'We'll give Tavi our present later.'

Mum looks like we've ruined her day and slumps onto the sofa. I glare at Ella. She shrugs, lowers her phone and casually walks out into the hall.

'Is that okay, Mum?' I say, waving yes to Milly and Anusha to follow Ella and Larissa.

'I wanted everyone to see it!' Mum says petulantly.

I squint at her. She's behaving like a teenager.

Dad says in the appeasing voice he uses when one of us, usually Mum, needs to relax, 'She can open our present with the birthday cake.'

'The birthday cake was next!'

'Here, drown your sorrows,' Ally says, handing Mum her Prosecco glass. 'Can't count the number of perfectly planned events I've had ruined by my kids.'

'It's okay, love,' Dad says, ushering me out. 'Head on upstairs.'

* * *

Milly and Anusha are sitting on my bed. Ella is collapsed on the bedroom floor, her whole body shaking as she cackles hysterically.

'Where's Larissa?' I say, shutting my door.

'Wardrobe,' Milly says.

'Larissa? Get out of my wardrobe.'

Larissa edges out, completely focused on the carpet.

'Are you ill?' I snap, no patience for Florence Nightingales.

Larissa pouts, shakes her head and shrugs a shoulder.

'Were you choking?'

Ella snorts and rolls back in renewed mirth.

'Right. So do you want to tell me what the hell that was?'

I look from Larissa, practically hugging the wall in the hope it'll absorb her, to Ella, who I now see is clutching my mystery birthday present to her chest.

'Did they really not guess?' Larissa says breathily.

Ella sits up and wipes her eyes with a dramatic sigh and snicker.

'Guess *what?*' I say.

Ella opens the case and displays the parts inside like it's a show-and-tell, and says, 'Want to guess what this is?'

'Not really. Think I've had enough games.'

'Is it a hair-remover thing?' Anusha says.

'Nope.' Ella looks to Milly.

Milly widens her eyes and shakes her head.

Larissa drops down onto my bed, behind Milly and Anusha, and hugs her knees up under her chin.

Ella wiggles the purple pebble thing and all its attachments in the air before her.

'I'm done with fucking games, Ella!' I snarl.

Ella glares at me. No one talks to Ella like that.

Then Larissa murmurs, 'It's a vibrator . . .'

LISS

Ella rolls her eyes at me. 'Spoil the surprise, why don't you!'

Anusha lurches off the bed. 'A what?'

'Did you just say—!' Tavi hisses, 'Vibrator?'

Ella makes it so much worse by dancing Tavi's present in the air, sing-songing, 'It's a vib-ra-tor!'

Tavi turns on Ella. 'You bought me a fucking *vibrator* for my birthday?'

'Yeah, well . . . you're single now and . . .' Ella falters. 'It was Larissa's idea.'

'What? It wasn't—' Oh, what's the point? I hug myself. This is horrendous.

'Mills, we should go downstairs,' Anusha says backing up for the door.

'Wait there!' Tavi points at Anusha, then to Milly who's rigid like a human shield on the bed before me.

If she goes, I'm following.

'Let me get this straight, Ella.' Tavi closes her eyes. 'You just let me open . . . !' But she can't even voice the rest of what unfolded downstairs.

'Yeah, well, that was unexpected.' Ella laughs. 'Honestly, the fact they were all filming too . . . !'

'Fuck you!' Tavi says, and goes to her door. But she doesn't storm out like I expect. Instead, she leans against the wood. 'Anusha,' she says quietly. 'Thanks for coming to my birthday. But let's be honest, you're Milly's friend, not mine. And now today's turned into a shit-show, I think it's obvious the party's over! Don't you?'

Anusha nods slowly.

'But . . . you know what,' Tavi adds. 'You've been a decent guest. Brought a nice – thoughtful – present. The kind of present that normal, sane people give someone for their birthday. So I'm going to be generous – maybe you, me and Milly can hang out sometime. Say hi to me in school, okay?'

Anusha gushes, 'That would be great!'

I can see Milly breathing now.

'Just one thing,' Tavi says, losing her smile and turning on an expression fit to kill. '*Do not* say a single thing – to anyone – about that present! Do you understand me? Not. A. Squeak!' She turns and glares at her sister. 'Milly . . . ?'

This time both Anusha and Milly nod, like their lives depend on it.

Tavi says, all sweetness again, 'Great! Okay, well, off you go. Tell your mum that you feel sick now too, Anusha, and you want to go home. We can blame it on the Tavi Tornados, can't we.' She opens the door, lets Anusha file out, and when Milly gets within touching distance, warns her, 'Don't you dare!'

'I won't—!' Milly says, and ducks out into the hall.

Tavi shuts the door firmly behind her.

Oh, sweet Mary . . . !

Tavi turns. Ella dives onto the bed and lies back against Tavi's pillows. I edge closer to the end.

Ella drawls, 'Thought you'd never get rid of the cling-ons!'

'Get off my bed, both of you!'

'Alright! Menstrual much?' Ella stands and tosses the vibrator beside me.

I recoil from the bed. 'Ella . . . !' But my voice dies in my throat when I catch Tavi's face. She's raging.

Ella protests, 'That's a really expensive vibrator, you know!'

'That mocktail,' Tavi says through her bared teeth, 'really *has* made you both sick, hasn't it! Party's over – go home.' She swings open the door and adds, 'And take that *thing* with you!'

CHAPTER 5

LISS

'You'd think we gave her a bag of dog poo for her birthday!' Ella says when we're nearly at the bus stop. 'Here, look, did you see the best bit?' Ella pushes her phone in my face and I realise she videoed everything too.

Anusha's writhing in the middle of Tavi's sitting room, rubbing the vibrator case all over her body. 'Ella! They *must've* known what it was!'

'Nah. Don't think so.' Ella slides forward through the video. 'This is where you come into shot – I might make a meme out of this bit.' She plays Tavi's mum slapping me on the back, rewinds it and plays it again.

'Enough,' I say, walking on.

'Aw, come on, you've got to admit—'

I stop. 'What are you going to do with that?'

'Hmm?'

'The video.'

'Nothing . . .'

'Ella! Please don't post that anywhere!'

'Why are you shouting at me? It was Tavi's mum's fault! Who plays pass-the-parcel after the age of five?'

As usual, Ella's shirking accountability. But at least she slides her phone into her rucksack pocket when we perch on the bench inside the bus shelter.

After a pause, I say, 'We should've taken it with us.'

'The vibrator? Why? I was being nice leaving it under her pillow! I don't think you realise how expensive that brand is. They're like the McLaren 750S of the vibrator world!'

I don't—

'It's a supercar – Maz is obsessed.'

'Right.'

'You're right though. I should've kept it for myself. She's so ungrateful! I mean . . . if one of us is going to have a vibrator it should be me! Considering Mum practically reviews them as part of her stand-up material. What do you think of Tavi's mum? Bit thirsty for the *socials*, don't you think?'

'She was okay . . .'

Ella mimics in a high-pitched voice, '*Hashtag Tavi's 17th birthday. Have a purple phlegm-flavoured mocktail!* And who invites Year Elevens to a seventeenth birthday to make it look like their daughter's popular? That's some seriously dysfunctional parenting right there!'

Inviting Milly's friend doesn't seem that odd to me. My younger brother, Jamie, brings his mates along to loads of our family functions. But that's not Ella's experience, I suppose. I'm tempted to point out that it might be Ella's own *dysfunctional* parenting that's led to her thinking giving Tavi a vibrator for her birthday was a good idea, never mind finding the resulting chaos funny. But why would I hurt Ella too? Two wrongs aren't going to make any of this better. I do have my concerns, though, that Ella's planning on posting that video somewhere, so I say, 'We can all feel lonely sometimes, Ella. Her mum probably invited more people to make Tavi feel better about Axel not being there.'

'Doubt it,' Ella grunts. But she doesn't say anything for a while, and I hope she's identifying with why Tavi was upset with us. Ella wouldn't like us embarrassing her in front of her mum or Maz either.

We get on the bus that passes both our houses and sit on the top deck. 'I can't believe Axel would tell Tavi that I called her a cock-tease and all those other *horrible* things!' I say. Adding, 'Do you think Tavi was lying? I know she's never liked me.'

'Lying? Why would Tavi lie?'

I shrug. 'It's just. Axel wouldn't say that about me.'

Ella exhales in a laugh but doesn't reply.

'Would he?'

Ella turns, all eyebrows skyward. 'Axel Mikkelson wouldn't blame someone else for something *he did*? Axel Mikkelson wouldn't try and manipulate his girlfriend to stop her hanging out with her friends . . . ?'

'But . . .'

'You know what he's like with Tavi. Everyone's seen it. In fact, he's like that with most girls! You're the exception. You're special. Well, you *were*. Because now he's blaming you for something *he's* said. Thing is, if Tavi *isn't* lying about all that, what else isn't she lying about . . .'

'What does that mean?'

'Perhaps the boy doth protest too much! It might be that Tavi being a cock-tease isn't the problem.'

I frown, confused.

'Axel can't get it up!'

'What?'

'Axel can't get a hard-on. Tavi let it slip. She said it was a joke after, but you can tell when someone's joking. Well, I can.'

'But. He. What do you mean he can't . . . ?'

'Get an erection?'

'Yes,' I say shortly.

'Oh, you're checking if I mean AXEL MIKKELSON CAN'T GET AN ERECTION WITH HIS PENIS?' Ella shouts to the top deck.

'Yess . . .' I hiss, burning with embarrassment.

'Yeah, well, she said he couldn't. And who tells people their boyfriend can't get hard? It's not exactly something you boast about. Could he get hard with you?'

I say nothing, but nod briefly.

'YOU MADE AXEL MIKKELSON HARD?'

Biting the inside of my cheek, I manage, 'Mhm . . .'

'That's obvious. You still do. Maybe that really is his problem. He still lurves you! Has he messaged you since he dumped Tavi?'

'No. He hasn't.' I look out of the bus window, hoping she'll lose interest in this topic. I don't want to tell her he messaged me this morning.

Ella lifts her mobile. And when I squint out of the corner of my eye, I see she's searching through vibrator reviews online. I focus out the window again and watch as the junction with Fairfield Road approaches. As we pass, I look down the road to the house with the scrolled, heart-shaped iron railings.

ELLA

Liss goes downstairs for her stop and I shunt along the seat to rest my head against the juddering bus window. I watch her step off onto the pavement below. She looks up and waves quickly, then sets off in the direction of her house. The double-decker passes her, and I crank my neck over my shoulder to watch her retrieve her phone and read her messages. Her ponytail flicks in and out of view. She's perky! Who's she perky about? Axel . . . ? Maybe just one of her *other* friends.

I open my phone and check my messages. Nothing from Liss. Not Tavi either. Maz? Miracles never happen. I go to the analytics for my channel. Five more unique users have viewed two of my videos. One wants me to use my feet in red jelly for my next ASMR video. Maybe I could do that with my hands . . . But not *red* jelly – it's too period-like. Blue jelly would look better . . .

I press the button and get off the bus. Walk to our electric gates. Type in the security code, slip in through the entrance and hike up the path through the trees.

'Hello?' I shout when I'm inside. 'I'm home!'

'Is that you, Eleanora?' Gran calls from the kitchen.

'Only me, Yaya. Has Mum left already?'

'About five minutes ago – I thought she'd forgotten something. Would you like one of your frothy coffees?'

'I'm fine. Want me to make *you* one?'

'Go on then.' Yaya clambers up onto a barstool – her hip must be good today. 'Were you at a party?' she says.

'Something like that . . .' I shove a coffee pod into the machine, put a glass mug below and press the button. 'How's your day been?'

'Oh, fine. It was fine . . . So the party was . . . ?'

The machine finishes and I set Yaya's decaf latte on its matching glass saucer and add a paximadia cookie on the edge. 'Eventful.'

'Were there boys?' Yaya asks, dipping her cookie in the milky top to soften it.

'No boys.'

'Shame.'

'We don't need boys for fun, Yaya! My gift was a hit.'

'If you say so.' Yaya leans forward and takes a tentative nibble. 'What was your gift?'

'A vibrator from Mum's comps cupboard.'

Yaya stares at me, paximadia between finger and thumb, and bursts out laughing. 'You didn't!'

'I did!'

'Oh, you're a wheeze, Eleanora!'

'I do my best,' I say, lifting my phone. 'I'm ordering takeaway. Want me to get you something?'

'No. Well, maybe a wee . . . Where are you ordering from?'

'McDonald's.'

She pulls a face. 'Have you any treats for me . . . ?'

'Might do . . . I made you frozen chocolate liqueurs. They're in the garage freezer.'

'Oh, you're a naughty girl, Eleanora! But I like you!'

* * *

I watch TV with Yaya until she dozes off. And once my food arrives, I go up to my room, unpack my six chicken nuggets, cheeseburger, ketchup and Diet Coke, flatten the paper bag out like a napkin and arrange everything neatly on top. I look up the first McDonald's mukbang video I can find and eat my food along with three girls chatting about their favourite dips. I should order BBQ sauce next time.

LISS

I wrap a hot, wet towel around my hair to set my Sunday night deep-conditioning treatment and settle on my bed to read through the chats on my phone. Eve from First Eleven Hockey's had her hair cut short and her boyfriend, Olly, hates it. I add my support.

Hockey Chat.

> **Me:** It really suits you, Eve! Brings out the green of your eyes.

I wait to see who'll comment next. I can see Ijeoma and George are typing but Ijeoma pauses and it's just George typing now. I flick out impatiently to see what my other messages are.

Axel Chat.

> **Axel:** Hey! Good Sunday? You free to video?

Why did I do that? If only I'd not opened his messages . . . Now he can see I've read this morning's too.

> **Axel:** You up to much today? Fancy go-karting?

I flick back to the First Eleven Hockey chat.

Hockey Chat.

> **Ijeoma:** Eve, bin the boy if he can't handle your beauty. Liss is right! (rainbow heart emojis)

I wait to see whether Ijeoma will write anything more.

> **Eve:** Aww, thanks, girls! (hearts of every colour).

I read through today's thread again and wait to see if anyone else posts. They don't, so I reluctantly close out and go to Axel's chat.

Axel Chat.

> **Me:** Hi, Axel. I had a good day, thanks.

I pause typing to touch my towel – it's cold now, so I lean down, grab my hairdryer and direct the hot air against the wet towel to warm it up while I type with my thumb, resting my phone against my knee.

> **Me:** Ella and I went to Tavi's birthday

Do I dare send him that? He shouldn't be messaging me. Not when they've just split up. Tavi's clearly gutted about it. But I need to gauge what's going on, and whether he said those things about me. Why would he say such horrible things to Tavi and blame me for it? Why's he dragging me into their drama? And after what Ella told me on the bus about him . . . Surely he's not still in love with me. It's well over a year since we split. I add:

> **Me:** party. Got to catch up on homework. See you in school tomorrow. Have a good evening! Liss.

In the morning, I'm distracted running out the door for school and don't check the time properly. So I arrive at the bus stop for the earlier bus, before my usual. I quickly scan the passengers inside as a couple of boys from school climb onboard and shake my head at the driver. The bus pulls away. I drop my bags on the ground and turn my phone onto selfie mode. Check my face. Close it again and flick through to my chats.

Ella Chat.

> **Ella:** Had an idea of doing a jelly ASMR. My ring light's glitching. Can you bring yours to mine tonight?

I sigh. I could jog back and get my light now but then I'll miss the next bus. I look down the street distractedly and flick to my other messages.

Hockey Chat.

> **Eve:** What surface are we running on tonight? What feet do I need?

> **George:** Spikes. We're on the track.

I grab my kit bag and rifle through its contents. My thumb feels the sharp nip of a spike inside my boot bag.

I pull them out, amazed that they're here. I don't remember packing them. But at least I don't have to go home now.

Ella Chat.

> Me: Can't tonight. I have a hockey run and social after. Could do tomorrow?

How did I forget the team run . . . ? My head's all over the place! I need to focus. Otherwise someone's going to notice.

ELLA

'Err, *morning, Liss!*' I shout to Liss's back after she walks straight past me outside school.

'Oh, hey, Ella. Sorry, I didn't . . .' She looks to her hockey girls like she'd rather just head on in with them.

'Don't let me hold you up!' I say.

'Hmm?'

'So . . . can you definitely bring me the ring light tomorrow night?'

'Yeah, I think so.'

'Liss! See you at lunch!' Ijeoma shouts at the gate, not even acknowledging me. Eve at least gives me a wave.

'Bye! See you later!' Liss waves like she's a little kid waving to passing cars. Her grin falls off when she looks at me.

'You can go with them,' I say. 'I wouldn't want to spoil your plans.'

'What? No. It's fine. I'm seeing them later.'

'Yeah, I know.'

'Are we going into school . . . ?' she says.

I sigh and walk. Liss follows.

'Did you get the English essay finished?' she says.

'Yeah.'

'I haven't yet. Could you have a quick look at mine?'

'Yeah, okay,' I say benevolently.

'Larissa!' a male voice calls behind us.

I turn to see Axel panting like a puppy. 'Hello, Axel . . .'

'Ella. Larissa . . .'

'Hi.'

'So . . . did you have a nice time at Tavi's birthday?' He quirks his mouth sarcastically.

'Yeah. Thanks,' Liss says.

Wait. How does he know Liss was at Tavi's . . . ? I purposefully didn't tell Maz what our plans were yesterday. I look between them. Oh, now you won't even look at me straight, Liss . . . ? You've been talking to Axel! I literally asked you—! 'Is Maz here yet?' I blurt to Axel.

'Uh. Don't know . . .'

'I'm gonna leave you two to it.' I toss over my shoulder, 'Keep your pecker up, Axel!'

CHAPTER 6

TAVI

'I'll keep it tucked under my shirt. We're allowed lockets and stuff,' I say, fingering my birthday gift from Mum and Dad – an amazing Tiffany & Co. dog-tag necklace with my initials engraved on it.

Mum pulls our car up in the usual spot beside the house with the topiary bushes she likes to post on Instagram. 'Where's Axel . . . ?' she says.

Shit. Of course she'd notice Axel's not waiting for me. 'Um, he's inside,' I mutter. 'He had to drop something at the . . .' I steel myself, waiting for Milly to put two and two together.

'Oh, there he is! Talking to Ella and that girl with the hair, Larissa. Ask them to tag photos from yesterday, will you?'

'What do you think Liss puts on her hair?' Milly says,

peering through the gap between the front seats. 'It's so . . . luscious.'

What are Ella and Larissa saying to Axel? Wait! What the hell? Now Ella's walked on and left Larissa alone with him!

'Tavi . . . ? Tavi!'

'What, Mum?'

'Could you follow your sister and get out, please?'

'Uh, right.' I open the door distractedly. 'Bye then.'

'Mills, good luck in your practical! Tavi – if I post birthday videos from yesterday will you repost them to your friends?'

'Okay.' I wave to Mum so that she'll leave. It works and I grab Milly by the blazer and drag her behind a tree. And peer round it. Larissa's got her back to me so I can't see what she's doing. But Axel's facing me and although he's swinging his school bag all relaxed, his face is bright red. Like he's embarrassed . . . ? No, now he's smiling. Sort of. Larissa flicks her long, blonde, *luscious* hair. Axel tosses his bag over his shoulder and shrugs, all chill and jovial. Larissa steps forward and Axel walks with her in through the school gates.

Fuck.

'What are we doing?' Milly says disdainfully.

'Nothing.' My heart is hammering so hard that I have to sit against the Topiary House's front wall and take deep breaths. I can't believe he'd go straight to her. The first day back at school after he dumped me. He was literally going out with me Friday school time! And she! After everything she called me. After coming to my house . . . And buying that birthday present with Ella!

I lean forward and the blood rushes to my head. Everything spins.

'You've broken up with Axel, haven't you.'

Ella *always* takes Larissa's side! It's like she sets out to purposefully mess with my head. *You don't have any other friends now Axel's dumped you, Tavi. So you, me and Luscious Liss can be frenemies together!*

'Tavi!'

I sit up. 'What?'

Milly's looking back down the street. 'Anusha's coming,' she says. 'Want to act a wee bit sane?'

'Hey there.' Anusha gushes at me, 'Hi, Tavi!'

'Hi, Anusha . . .'

She says uncertainly, 'You said I could say hi at school . . . ?'

'Yeah. It's fine.'

'I have the *worst* hangover after yesterday!' she says brightly.

'You don't look like it,' I mutter.

'Make-up!' She fans her long fingers across her fresh, totally-not-hungover face.

'You'll have to show me how to use that contour palette then,' I say distractedly.

'Definitely!' Anusha beams. 'The Tiffany tag necklace you got from your parents is beautiful. Really modern!'

I stand up, testing my legs. 'How d'you know I got that?' I take a few steps and the legs hold up.

'Milly posted pictures last night,' Anusha gushes.

'Where did you post pictures?' I glower at Milly.

'Don't worry! I put them on my Finsta. Maybe if you'd followed that account when you had the chance, you'd know that.' She crocodile-smiles sarcastically.

'Yeah, how have I survived without seeing your riveting posts about how much you love unicorns!'

'Unicorns?' Anusha says.

'You know I'm not into unicorns anymore, Nush!' Milly snips. 'Tavi's just being a grumpy bitch because it turns out Axel did dump her!'

Anusha gasps.

I glare at Milly, struggling with an overwhelming desire to strangle her scrawny neck. But instead of choosing sisterly violence, I head for the gates.

'Oh, I'm really sorry about Axel!' Anusha says, keeping up with me. 'What happened?'

'Nothing,' I say, looking over my shoulder to check the road's clear so I can step round the patch of pavement where Larissa stood with Axel – that tarmac's contaminated. 'Not that it's either of your businesses . . .'

'No. I mean, I wasn't prying. It's just . . .' Anusha's chattiness dries up.

I pause, realising she's distracted me enough that I've already passed through the school gates which will always now remind me of *him and her*.

Anusha takes this as an invitation to start talking again. 'Has *Axel* had his seventeenth birthday yet . . . ?'

'Yes. Why?' Then I realise she's just fishing for information because, like all of Milly's year, she worships older boys. I turn and head up the path. Anusha follows me for a few more steps before she finally gets the message that she's not invited.

'Um . . . bye, Tavi!' she calls. 'Your birthday present really is stunning!'

I nod and wave over my shoulder. Then remember darkly what my *other* birthday present was from Ella and Liss. Wait— Did Mum just say she's posting videos of my birthday? 'Milly—! Don't you dare repost Mum's videos!'

Ella clatters her tray down opposite mine at lunch.

Larissa better not be joining us! This morning's been torture enough picturing her and Axel snuggled up in Spanish while I had Chemistry.

'New necklace?' Ella says.

I tuck the dog tag in below my shirt again and stab my fork blindly into my chicken Caesar.

'You're not *still* mad about the vibrator?'

I check to see if anyone in the canteen's reacting to *vibrator* from canyon-mouth Ella. But the surrounding racket's deafening.

'In fact,' Ella says, 'give it back and I'll have it. I'm chucking Maz.'

'You're confusing me with someone who cares what you do, Ella.'

'So you *are* pissed!'

'Me? Why would I be pissed at *you*, Ella? I mean, it's not like you gave me a totally inappropriate present in front of my family! And it's definitely not like I found it shoved under my pillow when I went to bed last night either!'

'Fine. Be like that then!' Ella stands and dusts off her school skirt. 'Me and Liss were just trying to help a girl out. Wasn't our fault your lame-ass mum decided to play goo-goo-ga-ga pass-the-parcel and show-and-tell with a *vibrator*!' Ella shouts the last word, and finally gets her reaction. Year Nine boys snort and echo *vibrator*. Then Ella flounces away across the canteen, straight to Maz. Which means . . . Axel. Sitting opposite. He looks up, clocks Ella and, like he can feel me watching him, meets my eyes across the noisy room. I quickly focus on Ella, who smiles sweetly and leans down to whisper in Maz's ear.

She'd better not be telling him about that vibrator! I prod my salad again. Not hungry now. Don't look at him again. Stab crouton. Bounces off plate. Drop cutlery. Gather tray and bag, and head for the recycling bins.

'Good birthday yesterday . . . ?' Axel says, making me jump out of my skin. I'm trying my luck at winging it through a sample driving-theory test, sitting on the windowsill outside the Business and Economics classrooms.

'Yes . . .' My stomach screws up like scrunched paper. 'Thanks for your happy birthday message.'

Axel nods and gives me an awkward smile, rubs his neck.

I focus back on my phone and the next question. *What should I do if there's been an accident? Do I drive on . . . ?* 'Have a good weekend yourself?' I say, avoiding his eyes.

'Yeah, it was okay . . .'

'Good . . .'

'Tavi?'

I look at him. 'Yes?'

'We said— You said you wouldn't tell anyone about . . .'

I frown. 'About what?'

He tips his head to the side. 'You know, about me not—About you and me.' Head tip again. 'Why we broke up.'

I realise what he's talking about – the reason he dumped me. Because I'm apparently so repellent that he can't get a fucking hard-on! 'Yeah?' I say tightly. 'I haven't told anyone.'

'Right. So you didn't mention it to . . . anyone at the weekend?'

'At the weekend? Do you mean at my birthday?'

He shrugs. 'Any time over the weekend.'

He knows Larissa was at my birthday then. That's what he's worried about! That's why he's come to speak to me? To check I didn't tell Larissa! 'Let me think,' I say, pondering. 'Maybe . . . I mean, Larissa and Ella were talking about— And then there were *all* Milly's friends from Year Eleven . . .'

Red faced, he says, 'You serious?'

'I didn't say anything, Axel,' I lie. 'Why?'

'No reason. I'm just checking . . .'

'Well, now you've checked. And I'm trying to do a theory test so . . .' I look back to my phone and take ages to try and get the words on the screen to solidify into intelligible sentences. When he doesn't leave, I say, 'Was there anything else?'

'I've got a birthday present for you.'

'A present?' My annoyance deflates.

'I bought it before . . .' He shrugs in place of finishing the sentence with I *dumped you*.

'You don't . . . Thanks. But.'

'It's heavy. I'll bring it to yours Wednesday night after school.'

'Axel, maybe keep it for yourself?'

'I've got one already.'

'Oh.'

'Look. Keep it, don't keep it. I want you to have it either way, so . . .'

'Okay. Bring it over Wednesday then. You can pick up your hoodie and stuff.'

'Great.'

I bite my lip, uncomfortable. And gesture to my phone. I want to finish my test before it times out. I want him to leave me alone.

He nods. 'Wednesday then.'

'Wednesday,' I agree.

He walks away and I stare at my screen. It's already timed out, but I can't focus on braking distances anyway.

'Hey!' he shouts from along the corridor, making me jump again. 'How do you like your Tiffany necklace?'

'Eh, yeah. I love it!'

'David and Caroline thought the heart pendant,' he says, adding all smug, 'but I chose you the dog tag!'

I stare at Axel. He chose my necklace. He chose this

piece of metal round my neck. He chose a *dog tag* over a heart. I can feel it burning my skin, like it's branding me. I can't believe he's taking ownership of it. Of me. Again. He chose a dog tag? What does that make me? And I fucking hate that he thinks he can still use Dad's first name. Like my parents will still be on first-name terms with him now he's dumped me!

I smile, trying to mask that I hate him for always pushing my buttons. Always knowing how to get to me. And before the smile can falter, I look back to my phone. Don't react. That's what he wants. Do not react. But I can't help myself. 'Mum and Dad were right,' I call. 'I would've preferred the heart!'

CHAPTER 7

ELLA

'Are you sitting here or not?' I snap at Tavi, soon as she walks into Modern Studies. I've had enough of her ignoring me all day. She either wants my charity or she— Aww, shit, she's been crying. I pull out her usual seat beside me, and say, 'Ms Grierson wants us to write up our interview findings . . .'

She nods pathetically and slumps into her chair. Her face looks like a marshmallow. Apart from . . . 'You've not blended your contour,' I say.

'Where?'

'Just.' Aw go on, call me Mother Theresa . . . 'I'll do it.' I open my make-up bag and blend away the brown line beside her ear.

When I'm finished, she mutters, 'Thanks,' to the desk.

I lean in and whisper, 'Don't look now but Grotbag Gillespie's eating bogies off the end of her pen again!'

Tavi makes a half-hearted impression of vomming.

Louder, I project, '*HEUGH!*'

'Ella Konstantinou! Are you going to be sick?' Ms Grierson shouts from the front.

'Something stuck in my throat, mzz!'

'Well, try and dislodge it more quietly! You're on a *chatter warning*, remember.'

Yeah. Thanks for the reminder.

Tavi unpacks her things. I wait for her to finish, then slide our task sheet between us.

I have kind of missed her all day. 'You okay?' I say, because I'm being silenced by no one, especially not a power mad teacher.

Tavi nods and makes a start on answering each of the questions so we can add it to our report later.

I should be ignoring her. I was *seriously* generous with that birthday present. And that was mostly because Axel dumped her. How much more supportive does she expect me to be? She's better off without him anyway. This is the last thing I'm doing for her until she starts giving back to me.

I scribble on my pad and slide it across the desk: That new pizza place . . . ?

She writes: ?

I twist the page and write: Tonight.

She hesitates.

I add: I'll pay.

She's not biting. Why do I care? She normally blanks me outside school anyway – except when we double date with the boys. I'm doing her these favours, and is she grateful? If Liss didn't have that hockey social, Tavi wouldn't even get asked for pizza! I write one last thing: I need your advice on something important.

And there she glows. A literal glow-up. Transforming from dull to beaming, thinking I need her advice. Tavi writes: Pizza!

'So do you want to talk about things now or when we have pizza?' Tavi says as we walk down the high street.

'Shopping first!' I say. 'I need your advice on what to buy.'

'You need my advice on what to buy . . . ? So you don't want to talk about Maz or anything like that?'

'Maz? God no. Why?'

'Well, I thought there was something important . . . ?'

'I'll tell you who *does* need to talk – Olly Standish and Eve Tennant. I heard at lunch, they're having *problems*.'

'Eve and Olly are having problems?' Tavi says, incredulous that school's ultimate power couple are in trouble.

She's right. It's unlikely. Especially as I've just made that snippet of gossip up. But who knows – perhaps Eve's drastic haircut does indeed announce trouble in paradise. And maybe, through this fib, I'll get Tavi to open up about Axel.

'Yup!' I say, linking my arm through Tavi's to pull her along faster. 'You know,' I fake whisper. 'Crap sex!'

'Oh, right . . .' she says stiffly. She really does need to loosen up and use that vibrator!

'Pizza place is up that way,' I say deciding to leave the gossip tactic for now. 'We'll go after. Let's work up an appetite first.'

'So where are we going? What are you buying?' she asks.

'It's a surprise – very intimate. You'll love it. Close your eyes. I'll lead you there.'

TAVI

Ella leads me blind along the street a short way and soon I feel the warmth of heating and bright retail lights shining through my eyelids. I brush past some clothes rails as she quickly moves me through the shop.

I hear a woman say, 'Do you have the bodysuit in a fourteen?'

'I'll just check the back,' the shop assistant – I guess – replies.

Ella pulls me in through a curtain into . . . one of the changing rooms? I love it when she acts silly with me. It's usually when she's in a good mood. Those are the days I feel like she values our friendship. I wait for her to tell me what to do next.

'So what do you think I should get?' she says.

I open my eyes, let them adjust to the bright light and emit an involuntary squeak when they focus on a glittery, neon-pink willy.

Ella snorts and grabs my hand, pulling me towards the display shelves. She picks up a red lipstick. 'This colour would really suit you!' She pokes it at my mouth, and as soon as the lipstick makes contact with my bottom lip it buzzes.

I push it away and stagger back into the curtain cordoning off this illicit area of the shop, getting tangled.

'Ooh, look, it's a baby bunny! Shall I get the bunny?' Ella says, grabbing a pink, rubbery toy bunny and bopping it in the air like it's hopping towards me.

'I've only got the body in a size twelve!' the shop assistant says behind me. Which makes me lunge forward away from the curtain. I hold my finger to my lips, to tell Ella to shut up.

Having none of it, Ella drops the bunny onto the shelf and grabs a red thing this time. '*Luhl lull luu!*' She wiggles her own tongue along with the red tongue-shaped device at me. 'Euww, that one's weird!'

I nearly wet myself when the shop assistant pulls back the curtain. 'May I help you, ladies?'

'Eh, yeah. I want to buy a vibrator,' Ella says confidently. 'Can you talk us through each model? I mean, I like the idea of having the lipstick one in my make-up bag, very discreet, but I need to know that it's ethical, that it's not been tested on animals. All my make-up's animal friendly. And . . . on that matter. Is it really appropriate for a rabbit to give pleasure to a human being? That can't be right. Isn't that sort of bestiality?'

I can't believe Ella's saying this so brazenly. I can't believe she's doing this again to me!

The woman takes the tongue from Ella and sets it back on the shelf. 'I'd be delighted to help you ladies, if I can,' she says smoothly, giving our school uniforms the up and down. 'Just one thing . . . May I ask how old you are?'

'I'm seventeen,' Ella says, putting her hand on her hip.

'Then I'm afraid I have to ask you to leave this part of the shop.'

'Why?' Ella says.

'I can't sell you these specific items if you're under eighteen.'

'But I'm seventeen! I'm legal. I've had sex. A lot!' Ella says blushing.

'We're going anyway,' I say. 'We've got that restaurant booking – remember, Ella, at . . .' I can't remember the name of the pizza place. I can't even remember my name right now.

'No! I can legally have sex. I should be able to buy myself a vibrator if I want!' Ella's blush has upgraded to indignance.

'I'm not legally obliged to sell you a vibrator, miss – not until you're eighteen. Now, I must take care of my customer, so please let me escort you out.'

And to my and Ella's absolute mortification, the shop assistant lady holds open the privacy curtain screening off the vibrators section and ushers us like criminals out of the lingerie shop.

'It's sexist! The biggest pile of steaming, sexist shit in the entire universe!' Ella shouts for the tenth time, as we sit at the bus stop across the road. I was keen to walk onwards to the next stop but I think Ella's enjoying vocalising her disapproval as close to shouting distance as possible.

'You can have mine. Just stop shouting *vibrator* at the top of your voice – there's an old lady coming.' I stick the pizza box in front of Ella's face, hoping she'll get diverted by food. She's been ranting so much I decided a takeaway was safer than sitting in. And because I sent her to cool off outside, I was the one who ended up paying for our pizza. 'Take two bits,' I say generously, hoping multiple slices will properly silence her gob.

The old lady sits down beside me. Her ugly little dog sniffs the arm of my blazer.

I shove half a slice in my mouth and chew. Carbs are supposed to be good for shock and trauma, aren't they? They always make sweet tea for people after a shock. And carbs break down into sugars . . . And that, back in the sex shop, has to be the most horrifically embarrassing, squirm-inducing situation I've ever been party to. Well, perhaps the second-most embarrassing, squirm-inducing situation. Secondary to Ella and Larissa giving me a vibrator in front of my family . . . I'm rambling – definitely in shock.

'Did you know you can't buy a vibrator until you're eighteen?' Ella shouts past me, doing nothing for my nerves.

I stuff the rest of my slice in my mouth and side-eye to my right, hoping the old lady's deaf.

'Eighteen!' Ella says, lurching from the bench to stand in front of me.

'Are you speaking to me?' the old lady says in a clipped accent.

'Yeah! How can it be legal to have sex at sixteen but illegal to buy yourself a vibrator?'

Old Lady shakes her head and sighs, shifting her one-eyed dog so that he's facing Ella.

I want to apologise. But Ella will get mad at me for not

supporting her. I offer Old Lady the pizza box instead. She takes a slice. It's not like Ella's sharing the pizza with me anyway. And at least this'll stop me stress-eating, choking and Ella explaining to the inevitably fit ambulance guys – because, sod's law, it'll be guys – who come to save me, the retail laws on rubbery pleasure devices.

'I blame,' Old Lady says, while chewing, 'the patriarchy. Men like to control women's bodies. No matter how old or young. They don't like us to be in control of our own orgasms.'

Ella's mouth falls open.

I turn slowly to look at Old Lady. Her mutt pants happily.

'Mmm, that's really rather good,' Old Lady says. 'May I have another?'

I tip the box towards her and she takes a double slice. She chews contentedly with her mouth open.

We get on the next bus and leave Old Lady and her dog, *Benedict*, well fed – turns out she lives round the corner and wasn't even waiting for a bus.

We sit on the top deck in an adrenaline come-down silence until the stop before Ella's, then – unfortunately for me – she pipes up, 'Right, it's decided – we're all getting one – a vibrator. On principle!'

I stupidly bite. 'What principle would that be exactly?'

'Just because you've got one already! You're in a privileged position. You're armed.'

'Armed? They're not guns!'

'They are. They're symbolic weapons. Loaded.' She stands and nudges my legs. I shift them into the corridor so she can get out. She pauses, gripping the pole at the top of the double-decker's stairs. 'And every girl should be armed. In the war against the patriarchy.' Before she swings down the stairs, shouting back up to me – so that every random on the bus hears – 'No longer will they control our orgasms!'

CHAPTER 8

ELLA

Once I'm off the bus and at my gate, I message Liss.

Liss Chat.

> **Me:** Forget the ring light for tomorrow. I've got something BIGGER! Meet me in the common room first thing.

I'm almost at my front door when Liss replies.

> **Liss:** That sounds . . . BIG! Can come in early if you want?

> **Me:** Yeah. Cool. Meet me at 7.45.

I slam the front door and head up the stairs.

'Ella?' Mum shouts from the TV room – she's in for once.

'Yeah! I'm going to bed! I've got an early start.'

She comes out into the hall. I lean over the banister to make it look like I'm interested in what she's going to say. She says, 'I've got an early car picking me up too. I'm at Film City in Glasgow all day.'

'Are you staying over?'

'It's a one-day shoot but I was thinking I could go on to the Stand after – they asked me to judge a comedy improv.'

I shrug. 'Yeah. So you'll be back Wednesday afternoon?'

'Maybe evening. I might have lunch and go shopping with Auntie Eilidh Wednesday.'

'Okay. Is Yaya coming?'

'Do you want her?'

'Yeah. Course. If she wants.'

'I'll see if she's free.'

'Okay. Well, I'm going to bed. Buy me something in Glasgow.'

'Obviously. Night then!'

'Yeah, night.'

Up in my room with the door locked, I check my phone. Liss has replied.

> **Liss:** I can bring the ring light in whenever you need it. See you in morning. Lx

I start typing a reply and then delete it. I'll talk to her in the morning. I chuck my phone on my bed and go through to my bathroom. Have a pee. Turn on my shower. Strip. Get under the water. Lather up. Have a thought. Turn the temperature down so that it's barely warm. Remove the shower head from the high hook. Bollocks! The hose runs through this annoying circular loop up beside the soap tray so I can't stretch the shower head down low enough to use it for the purpose it's not intended. I can't believe I gave Tavi that vibrator. What a waste!

Although . . . maybe I can . . . I kill the water. Get a grip of the shower head and with slippery fingers unscrew it from the reticulated metal hose and, once separated, drop the metal snake back down through the loop so that the end now hits the shower tray floor. I retrieve it and reunite it with the shower head, screwing it on as tight as I can manage, and turn on the warm water jet again. This will do me for now.

* * *

'Morning!' Liss says, collapsing onto the beanbag beside me.

'Get me an espresso, will you?' I say. 'I'm gagging for caffeine.'

'Okay . . .' Liss rolls off the beanbag and practically skips to the machine.

I stop flicking through my phone and narrow my eyes at her. What's she so happy about? I watch her flip her hair. She's definitely used those gold tongs on it.

'Espresso?' She turns with the little mug in hand. 'Not a latte?'

'Espresso,' I say.

She looks back at the panel and wiggles her finger at the screen, looking for the option. She's singing to herself now.

'Double!' I shout.

'Blimey. You're really tired then?' she says brightly, slotting in the mug and prodding the screen.

'Knackered,' I mutter under my breath. I was absolutely buzzing first thing. Literally buzzing! After last night – I passed out straight after I came – I had to have another go of the shower this morning. I wish I could bring it with me to school. I need to get my own vibe ASAP.

'Here you go.' Liss hands me the mini mug.

'Thanks.' I down the shot. 'Right, sit. I need you to help me start a revolution.'

TAVI

'We need to talk!' Mum says, pushing into my bedroom in the morning.

I quickly pull my school shirt on. 'You couldn't knock?'

'You should be dressed by now.'

'Yeah, well, I didn't sleep that well.'

'Why?'

'No reason.' I fumble to close my last button and tuck my shirt into the waistband of my skirt. Turning, I say, 'What do we need to talk about?'

Mum's holding up a small, black foil square.

'What's that?'

'You tell me!'

'I don't know . . .' I move closer and squint at it. 'Where did you find it?'

'Douglas's basket. He's been eating it!'

'Is it a sweet wrapper?' I peer at the unopened packet punctured multiple times with Douglas's telltale teeth wounds. Across the square in hot-pink letters is *GLIDE*.

'It's lube, Octavia!' she hisses. 'Don't pretend you don't know what it is.'

'Lube?'

'Lub-ri-cant. Sexual lubricant.'

'Eww.'

'Yes, eww! And Douglas was licking it like a lollipop! I

know I said that you and Axel can . . . you know. But I warned you to be discreet – Milly's only fifteen!'

'It's not mine.'

'Then whose is it?'

'I don't know, Mum. But Axel and me broke up.'

'You— What? When?'

'Last Friday.'

'Why didn't you tell me?'

I shrug and mumble, 'I don't have to tell you everything.'

'But you're okay?'

I double shrug.

Mum looks at the packet in her hand, grimaces an *ick* face and quickly pincers it between the nails of her thumb and forefinger. 'Whose *is* this?'

'All I know is it's nothing to do with me. What about Milly?'

Mum's whole face flushes. 'Surely not!'

'Is it yours?' I say distractedly, because I kind of want to get ready for school.

'What? No! Douglas must've . . . picked it up on the street?'

'Ugh, gross! Get it out of here then!'

Mum squeaks and, holding the packet of lube at arm's length, runs out of my room.

* * *

I think I'm suffering from PTSD after what happened in that sex shop last night. That and I've finally accepted that Ella hates me. There was me thinking she was trying to make amends, going for pizza and needing my advice but it was all a trick to humiliate me. Well, I'm done! Even if she genuinely wanted to buy a vibrator, she could've been honest and asked if I'd go with her. Given me the choice. Why are people always manipulating me to do things *they* want to do?

I brace myself going into the Upper Common Room, and sure enough Larissa and Ella are deep in conversation on beanbags behind the pool table. Instead of straight up leaving immediately, I stupidly head for the drinks machine.

'Where are *you* going?' Ella shouts.

'Me? Getting a drink . . .'

'Get me a bottle of Irn-Bru.'

'Okay.' What the hell is wrong with me?

She beckons furiously. 'And hurry up! Liss? Want anything?'

Larissa smiles across the common room at me. 'Please can you get me a green tea, Tavi?'

'Err, yeah, okay . . .' Not only am I a simp, I'm also mildly dazed to find myself on the receiving end of *that* smile and 'please' from Larissa. It's the smile she uses for Axel and Ella or any other gullible human she wants to charm. Too tired to start a fight with Ella over what an utterly toxic friend she is, I gather the drinks together and bring them back to the seats. Yes, I am indeed, a simp.

'Right. Sit,' Ella instructs.

I narrow my eyes but sit.

'Liss is in, aren't you.'

'Potentially,' Larissa says. 'And everyone else is at least *interested* . . .'

I dare to ask, 'Interested in what?'

Ella elaborates, 'Getting vibrators. Obviously!'

Obviously. 'What do you mean *everyone else?*'

Ella shrugs. 'Liss messaged her . . . *connections*. We're starting a club! Are you helping?'

'No, I'm not.'

Ella glares at me.

I try to ignore her by taking a gulp of coffee, and scald my tongue. I can't believe they've told *everyone* about the vibrator. And what does she mean, a club? 'You know what, Ella?' I spike. 'I don't care! Genuinely. If you want to buy yourselves massive dildos that glow in the dark, I. Don't! Care! Whatever it is you're planning, it's nothing to do with me! Leave me out of it.'

Larissa's big blue eyes look ready to rupture.

'Morning!' I hear just behind me.

I crank round in my seat. 'Uh, yeah, morning . . .'

Axel's grin freezes when he clocks me. Which I can only pray means he *didn't* just hear me ranting about dildos?

And . . . hadn't realised I was sitting here? Which makes me look back to Larissa and Ella. They're both crocodile-smiling at him. Oh yeah, of course – Ella's shipping Larissa and Axel!

I slide my fingers below the chain of my birthday necklace, trying to stop it touching my skin.

After a moment of silence, Ella says, 'So how are we going to get them?'

I look up and realise Axel's already walked away, and both Ella and Larissa are staring at me expectantly. 'Uh . . . ?' I pull the dog tag out from below my shirt.

'How do we get everyone else a vibrator?' Ella says impatiently.

I swear, she's fetishising saying *vibrator* all the time. 'I don't know!' I say. 'Hasn't your mum got a box full of props and freebies you could raid?'

'To be fair, that *is* where yours originated but nah, the freaky ones end up in her secret sex-gadgets drawer. The others go in her stand-up act – and they're not very clean . . .'

I'm suddenly feeling the boaks coming on.

'Stop being so dramatic,' Ella snaps. 'I intercepted yours before Mum even received it. You know I steal my make-up from her sponsorship deliveries – so there's your proof. I even got that tape gun, so I can wrap the shit freebies back up and she's none the wiser!'

Ella has succeeded in mentally scarring me. I don't think I'll ever be able to speak to her mum without picturing her freaky-sex-gadgets drawer. 'So there's no more deliveries you can steal then?' I say weakly.

'No.'

'Right.'

'I might quite like one . . .' Larissa says quietly.

Course you might, I brood.

'So I've been thinking,' Ella says in that matter-of-fact voice she uses when she's about to manipulate someone. 'We're going to order a late,' she air-quotes, '*birthday present* for you, Tavi. Cause, you know, Larissa never bought you a present for your party and she felt *really* awkward and so I've generously offered to pay for her present *to you* and then Liss will pay me back!'

'I thought the vibrator was from you *and* Larissa? That's what you told me.'

'Yeah, it was.'

Larissa pipes up, 'I didn't have much say in the matter. Ella said—'

'Anyway!' Ella snaps – making me want to know what else Ella said about me to Larissa. After everything Larissa said about me! But then Ella info-dumps from a great height.

'I had a load of Amazon vouchers from my birthday so we've just used them to order everyone else a vibe too.

The delivery's arriving at yours tomorrow, so we need to come over after school to pick them up.'

I have a moment, staring at the space in front of my nose. Then I say, 'You've sent a load of vibrators to my house?' And then add because they don't say anything as rapidly as I deserve, 'Again! What's wrong with *your* house?' Which is a pretty coherent question under the circumstances. 'You've just told me that you intercept your mum's deliveries! You have a tape gun! Why didn't you send them to her? Or yourself even—?'

This seems to tweak Larissa's common sense because she looks slightly more thoughtful than usual and turns to Ella. 'That would have been a good idea . . .'

Ella just shrugs and says, 'They'll send us your one-hour delivery slot in the morning.'

'What're you up to today . . . ?' I say at breakfast next morning to Mum, all chill like I'm not really interested.

Mum's staring at the cooker.

'Mum?'

'Hmm?'

'Are you going to be at home today?'

'Yeah. Why?'

'Ehh . . . I was just wondering.'

'Is there a reason I shouldn't be here?'

'No! I just thought . . . Maybe you should go out. Out and about. Some fresh air. I dunno.' Ergo, get out of here so you don't peek inside my delivery of vibrators, like that time you *accidentally* opened your birthday present from Dad even though he'd ordered it in my name so you *wouldn't* open it! 'Why don't you surprise Dad at the garage and go out for the afternoon?'

'Surprise him? Do you think I need to surprise him?'

'Ehh, yeah . . . Maybe get dressed up. Look nice.'

She touches her hair. 'Do you think I need to make more effort?'

I laugh. But when she gives me eyes like Douglas used to when he was a new puppy and cared that we loved him, I say, 'Mum, you always look good! Well, except for when you have a hangover. And you look a bit bedraggled today. You okay?'

'Fine. Well . . .' She turns on her swivel stool and pours her coffee down the kitchen sink. 'You don't think that lube packet was Milly's, do you?'

'Mills?' I say, genuinely surprised that Mum's still worrying about that. She's not even got a boyfriend. I know I think of her as my baby sister, when she'll be sixteen next month, but still . . . !

'Forget it,' Mum says. 'You're right. Maybe I will see if your dad wants to go out for lunch. We could go to the cinema.' She yells, making me recoil, 'Milly! Hurry up, you're going to miss the bus—!' Her eyes settle on Douglas's empty dog basket, and she zones out for a moment. Douglas must see her too because he barks from the garden side of the patio door. 'Let Douglas back in, will you?' she says, snapping back into action. 'I'm off to have a bath.' And shouts from the hallway, 'If I do go out, you can invite Ella or that nice girl Larissa over for tea after school. And Anusha for Mills – keep an eye on her. Use my iPad to order yourselves pizzas!'

I suddenly remember what else is happening after school 'Shit—!' I grab my phone.

Amazon Delivery Chat.

> **Me:** Axel's coming here straight after school! You and Larissa need to skive classes during that one-hour delivery slot and get the

I glance guiltily over my shoulder to check Mum's definitely gone, and type:

> **Me:** vibrators.

Ella: Chill!

Me: Easy for you to say. You're not the one getting a bulk order of vibrators delivered to your house! How many HAVE you ordered?

Ella: Why's Axel coming to yours? You're not back together, are you?

Me: What's it to you?

Ella: That guy's so toxic! He's probably crawling back because he knows me and Liss were at your birthday and he's jealous.

Me: Toxic calling the kettle toxic!

Ella: Eh? Genuinely, I don't care if you're back with that douche. Just don't keep asking me to rescue you when he dumps you again.

Me: Glad to know where I stand, Ella. FYI he's just dropping off my birthday present. That he bought before he dumped me! It's obvious you're shipping him and Larissa anyway!

Larissa: We'll be there.

I freeze when I see Larissa's message. Ella's got me so riled I forgot I added Larissa to this message thread yesterday. I read through the argument again. Feel sick. And type.

Me: Thanks, Larissa.

CHAPTER 9

LISS

I remove my AirPods, slot them into my blazer pocket and squeeze between the school bags and bodies packing the bus. 'Hey . . .' I say, smiling.

'Hey.' Ijeoma flips her headphones down so they rest round her neck.

I steady myself, holding onto the metal bar as the bus pulls away. The collar of her white shirt's caught inside the cup of the headphone. I want to straighten it.

'What time are they getting delivered?' Ijeoma says.

I feel myself blush. Why do I always blush? 'I don't think Ella's been given the time yet.'

Ijeoma nods. The bus accelerates and we both grip the same bar. There's barely standing room and other kids keep bashing against my back and legs.

I bite my lip. 'So . . .' I say. 'You think it's a good idea?'

I nod, not really wanting to go into further detail about what Ella's got planned, here on the bus with younger years around us.

'It's a brilliant idea. I might've preferred to choose my own, but I'm interested to see what you chose me.'

Yet more blushing. 'Ella chose some too . . . We ordered a variety. I can ask for you to have first pick, if you'd like?'

Ijeoma's mouth quirks. 'You probably shouldn't have told me Ella chose some.'

'Oh, no . . . Really?' I sigh. I knew she'd be funny about Ella. They all would.

She smiles. 'It's alright. I'm chill. I'll pretend you chose it—' The bus brakes suddenly and she's flung up against me with the momentum. 'Sorry!' she says, touching my arm apologetically as she moves away.

'That's okay,' I say, my skin prickling below my sleeve.

Ijeoma grins. 'We might make it to school in one piece if we're lucky.'

I grin too. But can't think what else to say.

The bus sighs and lowers. And I realise we're at the next bus stop.

Her eyes slide over me, past me.

I turn to look towards the driver.

George is at the front, waiting to swipe her phone on the reader. She waves.

I wave back. Keeping my eyes locked on her, while my every cell is acutely focused elsewhere.

And finally, George manages to push her way through all the younger kids to hold onto *our* bar *between us*.

TAVI

'If Miss Cranston realises I'm not in the editing suite,' Ella mutters after lunch, as she, me and Larissa crest the hill before my house, 'I'm on detention, you realise?'

I say, 'And that's my concern how?'

'You're very uptight,' Ella says. 'You obviously haven't used your vibrator yet—'

'Girls! What are you doing out of school?'

I jump out of my skin at Mum, who's pulled up beside us in the car.

I side-eye Ella and Larissa, and back to Mum. Did she hear Ella say the V word? Do not say the V word again, Ella!

Larissa unfreezes first. 'Um, Tavi has a del—'

Shut—! 'We've been sent out to research . . .' I scan our surroundings desperate for inspiration, 'bins.'

'Yeah, it's an environmental project,' Ella says easily. 'You know, to check the local council's supplying enough recycling . . .'

'There's one!' Larissa squawks, and fakes adding another bin to the imaginary tally on her phone with a flourish.

I blurt at Mum, 'You've not been out for lunch already, have you?'

'No. I'm going to pick your dad up now. We're going to the cinema afterwards. Why?'

'No reason. I was just wondering . . .'

'Have *you* had lunch?'

'Yes – but is there food at home?'

'In the freezer,' she says, glancing in the rear-view mirror, then her wing mirror. 'I said you can order pizzas if the girls stay for tea. Just make sure Milly travels straight home from school, and don't feed Douglas again! He's been fed and I don't want to clean up his puke when I get back. Or anyone else's for that matter,' she adds warningly. She glances over her shoulder, pulls into the road and calls, 'Behave!'

Larissa looks at her phone and says, 'It's one minute past two.'

'Shit!' I swing my bag over my shoulder and run.

'These things never arrive on time!' Ella yells after me. 'We haven't even seen a delivery van go past.'

'It might've come from the other direction!'

Ella and Larissa catch me up and we arrive breathless at my house five minutes into the delivery window. We let ourselves in and thankfully there's no SORRY WE

MISSED YOU note on the doormat in the hall. Douglas barks from the kitchen and pelts through to do a circuit around Ella and Larissa. And the girls head to the family room to collapse on the sofa. Douglas jumps up between them, ready to be worshipped. 'Can we order pizzas now?' Ella says, looking round the room as if she hasn't seen it before.

'They'll take too long – I want to head back to school if it arrives soon,' Larissa says. 'What about toast?'

'Bread bin's over by the kettle,' I say, inspecting a cardboard box sitting on the sideboard. It has Dad's name on it. Wondering how far Ella might take her sadistic pleasures of messing with me – would she send the vibrators to Dad for shits and giggles? – I say, 'You definitely addressed the package to me?'

'Yup,' Ella says, distractedly looking through her phone.

I try to lift the box just to be sure, but it's so heavy I can't even shake it. It must be a car part. So I go to the kitchen to show Larissa where the butter and jam live.

Larissa and I make a batch of toast and we all sit on the sofa scarfing it down and impatiently watching the big clock over the cooker. This is weird. Having Larissa in my house twice in one week. All of the things Axel told me she called me. *Cock-tease. Skank. Cheap.* I scan our living area. Has she got a massive house like Ella? Do they both think I'm low grade and that's why they're constantly trying to humiliate me? Is Axel in on it? Are all three of them working together to fuck with me?

'Oh, that's a lovely necklace!' Larissa says.

I look down, realising I'm gripping the dog-tag pendant. 'Eh, yeah. My mum and dad gave me it for my birthday.'

'Tiffany,' Ella says knowingly.

'Eh, yeah,' I say.

'Wow!' Larissa says. 'Gorgeous. Is that your initials?' She leans closer and her hair falls over my arm.

'My real name's Octavia,' I explain stiffly, looking at the perfect, curled locks of golden hair.

'Octavia,' she repeats. Releasing the dog tag and giving me airspace in one move. 'What's your middle name?'

'Isla.'

Ella snorts. 'Well, they weren't going to put T for Tavi as the first initial, were they!'

Larissa frowns and then it dawns on her. Yeah, my last name is Thompson. So at least this literal dog tag that my then boyfriend picked out for me doesn't have TIT written all over it. Even if my forehead seems to.

At ten to three I say, 'Check your emails, Ella. In case they've sent you a new delivery slot.'

Ella sighs and flicks through her phone. 'Oh . . . it says it's been delivered!'

'No, it hasn't!' I say, skating on my tights through to

the hall to open the front door. There's nothing sitting on the doorstep. Nothing hiding behind the wheelie bins. Nothing under the doormat. I slam the door and leg it upstairs. No packages on my bed. Nothing sitting in Mum and Dad's room. Not in the hallway. The kitchen. Nothing . . . 'Shit!'

'What?'

I lift the white card from the middle of Douglas's bed. *SORRY WE MISSED YOU. We Tried To Deliver Your Package Today. Time 14.01. Left It With Your Neighbour. No. 23.* 'Oh, thank God! Next door has it!'

I shove my feet into my school shoes and troop out into the street and back down next door's pathway and ring the doorbell. I can hear Petal, their cocker spaniel, barking in the hall. I wait for what seems a long time. I ring the doorbell again. And again. Petal keeps barking. I peer in through the side window and can just make out a cardboard box sitting at the foot of the stairs. Petal jumps up at the window and snaps. She's vicious. Her owner, Mrs Stanton, isn't much friendlier. She let rip into Mum one time we strung fairy lights in her tree's branches, overhanging our garden. Said we had no right to touch her property.

I go back into my house.

'Where is it?' Ella says.

'Next door.'

'And?'

'She must've gone out. Why didn't you check your emails before now?'

Ella makes a whiny mocking face. 'Because I didn't.'

Douglas moans at the patio door. I go over and slide it open to let him out.

'How long will she be?'

'How should I know!'

'Well, where's the package?'

'In the hall, I think.'

Ella groans. 'I need to get back – haven't you got a key? Sarah next door to us has our key, and we have hers.'

I blink. 'Oh, we do!' I open the second drawer down from the cutlery drawer and search through the instruction books and guarantees for the brown envelope that Mum put the neighbour's key in. Only the envelope isn't here. 'Damn it! Mum probably gave it back to her – they had a fight.'

'What about windows, has she left any open?'

'Not at the front . . .' I walk out into the garden and drag the garden table over towards the fence. I climb up and look over. 'I can't see any open . . .' Ella and Larissa join me on top of the table.

'There,' Larissa says. 'That window looks ajar.'

She's right. One of the little high-level windows on the side of the conservatory looks like it's not been shut properly.

Ella squints. 'Too narrow.'

Petal appears in the conservatory and barks rabidly.

'I'm out,' Ella says. 'The ankle-biter looks lethal.'

'She hates females except Mrs Stanton. Douglas on the other hand . . .' Douglas licks his chops and continues panting up from the patio at us. 'She loves him.'

'That window up there's open too . . .' Larissa points to the side window on the first floor between our houses – next door's bathroom. 'Have you a ladder?'

'Well, yeah. Huge ones in the shed.'

'Safe ones?'

'Course. Dad's got all the kit. There's harnesses. We used them when we cleaned out the gutters in the autumn.'

'Do you really want to do this?' Larissa says to Ella.

They exchange a look.

'What about the midget beast?' Ella says, tipping her head towards Petal, who's standing on the back of an armchair baring her teeth at us.

Larissa grimaces.

Ella points her thumb towards Douglas. 'So she fancies Doug the pug?'

'Douglas,' I say automatically. Mum goes ballistic when anyone shortens his name to Doug. But I answer Ella. 'She does.'

'Whadya say, Duggie Boy?' Ella says looking down at him.

Douglas whines then barks.

Weakly, I protest, 'Why don't we wait for Mrs Stanton to come back? She might return any minute!'

Ella sighs. 'Fine. I'm heading back to the editing suite then.' She jumps off the table. 'You can bring the vibrators into school tomorrow.'

'But . . . !' I look at my phone. 'Axel will be here in an hour.'

Ella rolls her eyes. 'Get the ladder and harness then.'

I pause, suddenly remembering that Mrs Stanton's a lollipop lady. Mum laughed about it to Dad. Said it was like Cruella de Vil working at Battersea Dogs & Cats Home. 'She won't be back for at least an hour,' I say to psych myself up. If I don't get the parcel now, then Axel will be here by the time she comes back. And she'll probably come round and ring the doorbell when she knows I'm back from school. And if Axel sees the package then he'll make me open it! And if I don't he'll think it's something I don't want him to see. Which is exactly what it is – something I don't want him to see . . .

Ella says, 'I'm starting a revolution, Tavi!'

'The ladder's in the shed.'

We drag the telescopic ladder out and carry it, between the three of us, along the side of the house. I show them how to ratchet it longer and then, shakily and unsteadily, we prop it up against our side wall and tip it backwards so it comes to rest just below the open first-floor window of next door. 'Maybe wedge the bottom against our wall so it doesn't slip . . .'

'Right, Tavi. Go out front on the road and watch for your neighbour. Call Liss if she comes back, then you call me, Liss. And push the ladder base right up against the fence and tip the top back against Tavi's house. That way she'll think someone's washing Tavi's windows.'

I pull an impressed face. This could actually work.

'But what will you do if I've moved the ladder?' Larissa says.

'Unlock the back door . . . ? Fall out that little window . . . ? She doesn't have a burglar alarm, does she?'

'I guess not, if Petal's there . . .'

'Petal?'

'The beast.'

'Could be one of those pet-friendly alarms. I might have to crawl about like the dog until I can see if there are sensors. This Petal, how much does she love Doug? Are we talking roll-over-and-show-her-belly-submissive-wifey sort of stuff?'

'Pretty much.'

'Sweet.' Ella pulls on the safety harness.

Larissa grips the empty ladder like her life depends on it. Ella's does. 'Ella,' she says, 'are you really sure about this?'

Ella lifts Douglas and tucks him down the front of her school blouse, and buttons up her cardigan. She answers, 'Hell, yeah!' and clipping her harness onto a higher rung, climbs up to meet it. 'Tavi, get out the front!'

I run along the alleyway, undo the combination padlock and pull the gate shut behind me so no one can see along our side. The street's empty. I walk further out into the road to see if anyone's coming. It's just after three. Most parents will be at school pick-up. I look back towards the house and Ella's already below Mrs Stanton's bathroom window. I can just see Douglas's little head popping out of her cardigan. Bet he's in ecstasy. He's a total perve for the girls. Ella pulls the frosted window open wider and leans in. I realise she's letting Douglas down first. Then she straightens up, and climbs inside . . .

I hear barking. Terrifying barking. And then silence. *If Petal's mauled Douglas because of a box of vibrators!*

CHAPTER 10

ELLA

When the barking subsides, I climb out of the neighbour's bath onto the tiled floor and creep to the door to listen. A muffled yelp and scuttling paws downstairs. If that nippy bitch eats Duggie Boy, Tavi's gonna kill me.

I step onto the landing and pause, remember there might be a burglar alarm and drop to my knees. I crawl across the cream carpet and peer down into the hallway. The carpet's synthetic. It's got that squeaky feel to it. And now my school tights have static white fluff all over them – if this gives me a rash! Another yelp and a snappy bark downstairs. Is that a good or bad thing? Dogs are such idiots. I swing my legs round and slide feet first down the stairs. The things I do for feminism . . . My skirt'll be worse than the tights. This is like *Mission: Impossible*. Just call me . . . I fish my phone out of my bra and turn on the video.

'Something . . . a little different today,' I whisper breathily to camera. 'I'm on a secret mission. Come with me as I try and retrieve a precious package. Sooo precciouss . . .' I hiss quietly in my best ASMR voice and rest my index finger against my lips. 'Shhh, we've got to be quiet . . .' And turn the camera round to face the Amazon box beside the front door as I bum-shuffle down the stairs. On the bottom step I hear a bark. I freeze. A low growl. My heart stalls. I wait for the neighbour's beast to come into sight. Still holding my phone filming. But then I hear a slightly deeper bark and another. I lurch for the box, swipe it – and scramble back up the stairs.

TAVI

A man and a little kid in a scarlet school jumper appear on the horizon.

I edge over to our side gate and open it.

Larissa's still holding the ladder.

'Do you think Ella's okay?' Larissa says, looking terrified.

'Hope so!'

We both look up at the window. And suddenly a large, flat Amazon box missiles out of it and crashes to the ground.

Ella climbs out, closes it behind her and makes her way down the ladder.

'Where's Douglas?' I hiss.

She shakes her head.

'What does that mean? Has she mauled him?'

'He wouldn't come. I called him, but I didn't want to alert the beast to my presence.'

'You can't just leave my dog behind!' I shout.

'He had to take one for the team.' She smirks.

'Ella!'

'Tavi! I'm pretty sure he's absolutely fine.' Ella jumps off the ladder a couple of rungs before the bottom, and quickly she and Larissa jiggle the base towards the fence like we planned and tip it back against my house. We lower it to the ground. 'Go and look round the back,' Ella says, brushing fluff off her knees and skirt.

I rush to the garden table and climb up again. Larissa and Ella join me.

'Go, Duggie Boy!' Ella snorts, holding her phone aloft to film.

My pug isn't quite taking one for the team so to speak. The randy little fucker's giving one out for the team instead. He's humping Petal on Mrs Stanton's favourite conservatory chair.

* * *

'That's got to be chafing by now,' Ella says unwrapping a miniature Mars bar while leaning on the top of our garden fence.

'Ugh, this is wrong,' I repeat.

'Can't take my eyes away, though,' Larissa admits, screwing up her empty Bounty wrapper and dropping it into the Celebrations bag.

'Do you think they're stuck,' I muse. 'What if his dick's stuck and they're actually trying to escape?'

'They're randy, Tavi. He's a randy little pug. And she's a horny beast.'

'Doggy style isn't exactly intimate, is it . . .' Larissa says quietly.

I side-eye Larissa, wondering for the hundredth time if she and Axel really did have sex. I know Axel told me he'd never had a problem getting hard before me. Told me I wasn't the first person he'd shagged. That other people enjoyed doing the stuff he wanted me to do. But if Larissa doesn't even like doggy style . . .

'I've always enjoyed it myself,' Ella says. 'It's animalistic.'

'We need to put the ladder away,' I say.

Ella squints her mouth condescendingly. 'You're never going to talk about this sort of stuff, are you?'

'What stuff's that, Ella?' I say defensively.

'Sex stuff.'

'Do you blame me?' I say, breaking my death-glare on

Ella to throw one Larissa's way. Why would I tell Ella and Larissa about my sex life when one's calling me cock-tease, skank, cheap, messy . . . And the other's constantly baiting me. Giving me vibrators. Telling me I'm better off without my toxic boyfriend and then doing her best to set him up with his ex—

'Uh, girls,' Larissa says. 'What's Tavi going to tell her neighbour?'

'About Douglas?' I say.

'No, the package. The last time the neighbour saw it, it was in her house. Now it's gone. And Douglas is there instead. Don't you think she'll put two and two together?'

'Nah.' Ella dips her hand into the Celebrations bag and grabs a couple. 'Got a packet of dog treats, Tavi?'

'Uh . . . probably.'

'Go get it then.'

Larissa and Ella take the ladder back to the shed for me while I search through the cupboards to find a full bag of dog treats. When I go back outside, Ella has the garden rake. She rips into the Amazon package, tearing part of the lid loose, fishes out a rainbow of slim rectangular boxes . . . eight of them! Hands the armload of vibrators to Larissa with the delivery note and climbs onto the garden table again. Ella leans right over the fence, hooks the barely open high-level window to the conservatory with the metal prongs of the rake and pulls it open. She then tucks the bag of dog treats into the Amazon box, under the brown packing paper, hooks the open box over the handle of the rake and reaches out into next door's garden to prod the box in through the open window, and pushes the window shut again.

'My work here is done,' Ella says, brushing her hands off.

Larissa and I watch in awe as Petal and Douglas immediately separate and go for the box that's fallen onto the sofa. Like a tag team of hyenas, they tear the cardboard and the bag of dog snacks to shreds, gulping up every last morsel.

And then, just as Mum predicted, Douglas pukes on Mrs Stanton's sofa. And Petal, the submissive wifey that she is, without the slightest batting of an eyelid, or turning up of her evil little wet nose, goes and licks it all up. Every stinking, boak-inducing drop.

'Gross!' Larissa and I say in unison.

'And that, ladies,' Ella says, 'is true love right there!' And jumps off the table, just as our doorbell rings.

CHAPTER 11

TAVI

'I thought we were walking back together from school?' Axel says, lugging a heavy box past me and thumping it onto the floor by the coat stand.

I glance over my shoulder and catch Larissa peeping round the door frame from our family room.

'Larissa?' Axel says. He flushes beetroot and glances uncertainly between us.

Larissa lurches forward like she didn't intend to, which means Ella probably pushed her, and says, 'Hi. Axel! How are you?'

'Eh – fine. What are you doing here?' He includes me in the question.

Larissa looks back for help.

Ella steps out into the hallway. 'Hey, Axel. Yeah, we were just doing a research project.'

'On bins,' I say, hearing how ridiculous I sound.

'Bins?' Axel says, rightly unimpressed.

'Anyway, best be going,' Ella says, ducking back into the family room to emerge stuffing a purple-edged slim box into her school bag. And I realise she has another yellow-edged box wedged under her armpit. 'Axel will have to help you look for Douglas,' Ella says pointedly as she passes us for the door.

'Uh-huh,' I say distractedly, eyeing the box for any telltale pictures.

'Yeah, he probably hasn't gone far.' She waves the box at Larissa. 'Come on, Liss, less of your dawdling!'

Larissa bundles up her blazer and school bag and flicks her luscious locks seductively. 'See you tomorrow, Tavi.'

I watch her closely as she passes me. Waiting for a surreptitious, telling glance towards Axel. But she just keeps her eyes downcast.

'Umm, yeah, tomorrow!' I say, as Ella and Larissa pile out of the door and slam it behind them.

'You're hanging out a lot with Larissa . . . ' Axel says.

I don't reply. I don't need to explain myself to him anymore. 'Shall I open my present?' I say.

He smiles. It's the smile that always made my tummy flutter. And like one of Pavlov's well-trained dogs, it does a backflip now. 'I need to go for a waz first,' he says. 'Get us drinks, will you?' And he jogs upstairs to the loo.

I'm not Axel's servant either, so I rush out to the back garden and climb onto the table to see what's happening. Douglas and Petal are now curled up on Mrs Stanton's favourite chair having a post-coital snooze. I should've got Ella to try the back door . . . Although she could be right and there's an alarm. I've heard a loud beeping noise on occasions, but I've always thought it was that guy with the van backing up out on the road. I guess Douglas will have to face Mrs S's particularly shrill brand of music alone on this one.

I head back inside and sit on the sofa. Axel still hasn't arrived back from the loo so I wander out into the hall to see if I can move his birthday present into the living area. But the box isn't there. 'Axel?' I shout.

'Yeah! I'm up in your room!'

He went into my room? Without checking with me! I run upstairs. I don't even know if there's anything embarrassing out. The vibrator should be under my bed. But Douglas was here on his own earlier. And I can't remember whether my bedroom door was already ajar when I was looking for that Amazon delivery. Please let the vibrator be hidden!

At the door, I shove a pair of pants that didn't make it properly into my laundry bin down below a sports bra and scan the room. The vibrator was in the neoprene case. Even if Douglas has dragged it out, surely Axel won't look inside. It could be anything. A make-up case. Anything. 'Oh!' I finally say when I realise Axel's staring at me expectantly and I follow his eyes to the top of my chest of drawers. He's gone ahead and unwrapped his present for me.

'Is that a good "*oh*"?' he says.

'Yeah. I mean. Wow. A turntable. I don't have any vinyl . . . but Mum and Dad might. Well, they've got CDs but . . .'

'There's that vinyl place on the high street. Beside the kebab shop.'

'Is there?'

'Some of it's expensive but they always have a deal on, and they've got a bargain bin.'

Axel flips open the clear lid of the record player turntable and shows me how to set the tonearm so it'll play and return at the end of the record.

'There's one problem,' he says. 'You need speakers.'

'Oh.'

'I couldn't afford them too.'

'Axel . . .' I realise that I can't accept this. I was too intrigued to think properly, but this is way too generous a gift now we're not together. Way too generous if we were still!

'I thought David would know somewhere to get speakers cheap,' Axel says smoothly.

'Dad will help – but you should keep this for yourself . . .'

'You know I've got a much better one. I thought you'd like it!'

'I do.'

'Well then. Have it.'

'Axel . . .'

'I think we should try again.'

'What?'

'We should try and work things out.'

'But—'

'You haven't told your parents we broke up, have you?'

'Well, I . . .'

'Come on. You and me. You know we're meant for each other.' Axel moves towards me.

I back up towards my bed and sink onto the mattress. Scrub at my forehead with my palm. 'I . . .'

He steps closer. 'You know it.'

'You were right on Friday,' I say. 'We need different . . . things.'

Axel kneels down in front of me, picks up my hand in his. 'You don't really think that, do you?'

Don't I? I don't know what I think. 'What were you saying to Larissa on Monday morning?'

'Monday morning?' He frowns.

'At the school gates.'

He shrugs. 'Nothing.'

'I saw you flirting!'

'Look. I wasn't going to say anything but seeing she was here earlier, and she came to your birthday. I don't think you should hang out with Larissa anymore. She's a bit . . .'

'A bit what, Axel?'

'Obsessed. She asked me out Monday and I had to turn her down. I don't think it's healthy for you and her to be friends. She's already got you paranoid and imagining things are going on between her and me. She wants to split us up.'

'*You* split us up.'

'You know what I'm like with commitment. My dad leaving . . . It's hard for me. I got scared.'

'But, why would Larissa . . . ?' I trail off because I know why. I came between her and Axel. Even Ella's made it obvious she wants them back together. I say, 'You absolutely promise you're not into Larissa anymore?'

'Fuck, no!' he laughs. 'She's too skinny. You know I like muscle on my girl's arse . . . !' Axel lifts my fingers and kisses my knuckles. 'Admit it, you miss me.' His blue eyes are locking me in place.

'Tavi!' Milly shouts from downstairs. 'Are you home?'

'Yeah!' I call back. 'Mum's gone out with Dad!' I extract myself and go to open my door. I need space. Air to breathe.

Milly's on the stairs. I step out onto the landing and pull the door behind me. 'Axel's here,' I murmur.

'Oh.' Milly pauses, holding onto the banister. She points, mouthing, *Want me to go back down?*

I shake my head. 'He's bought me this expensive birthday present.'

'That's nice!' She comes up, pushes my door ajar and waves briefly. 'Hi, Axel!'

'Hey, Mills! You good?'

'Yeah. Good, thanks.' She looks at me. 'I'll take Douglas for a walk . . . ?'

'Eh – you can't.'

'Why?'

'He's fine. He's just a bit, *busy* . . .'

'Busy with what?'

'Axel, give us a sec.' I pull my door shut again and tug Milly by the arm to follow me downstairs. I go out into the garden, climb up onto the garden table and point. Milly follows me.

'How did he get in *there*?'

'Long story. Don't tell Mum and Dad.'

'Cruella'll do her nut. *She'll* definitely tell them.'

'Yeah. Unless we can break him out of there before she gets home . . .' I glance up the side of the house to the corner of my windowsill.

'Are you and Axel back together then?'

'I don't know.' I get down off the table and walk to the patio door. 'Maybe.'

'You don't seem very happy about it.'

I shrug, thinking I'm not even sure what happy is anymore, but say, 'Mum said we can order pizza.'

'Result!'

ELLA

'What's really happening between you and Axel?' I say to Liss when we're waiting for the bus.

'Nothing. I've told you.'

'Yeah, I know you said that but I'm never sure with you.'

'What's that supposed to mean?' Liss snaps back.

'You said you hadn't spoken to him lately. But you had. Hadn't you!'

Liss exhales, then lies, 'There is absolutely *nothing* going on between Axel and me.'

'Hmm, maybe not yet . . .'

'Are you taking all of those things home or shall I take some?' she says, gesturing to the boxed vibrators in my open bag. She's trying to divert me.

'No, I can manage. Wouldn't want to put you out.'

Liss sighs again. There's something going on she's not telling me. I know it.

I offer, 'You can pick yours now.'

'No, I promised— Uh . . . I'll pick mine with the others.'

'Yeah?' I side-eye her. 'Suit yourself.' There, she's acting like a weirdo again. We sit staring at the tarmac, then I say, 'So you're not bothered if Tavi gets back with Axel?'

'No. I'm really not. I don't want dragged into their drama.'

'If you say so . . .' More tarmac gazing. 'You *definitely* don't like him?'

'I don't.'

'Fine. That's that then . . . Do you like anyone else?'

'No.'

'No one?'

'Nope.'

'Hmm . . .' I inspect my gel nails. 'What's Eve Tennant done to her hair?'

'I think it's nice. It brings out her eyes.'

'It's rank. Do you think Olly'll dump her?'

'For cutting her hair?'

'No. Crap sex.'

'What?'

'Never mind. Send out the invites for tomorrow, will you? We'll meet in the dance-studio changing rooms during lunch.'

TAVI

'I've missed this arse!' Axel says, rolling me on top of him and grabbing a hold of my buttocks under my school skirt. We're lying on my bed kissing.

'That's a bit sore . . .' I say, trying to loosen his gripped fingertips.

'But they're just so kneadable . . .' he says, digging his fingers in deeper. I'll have a fan of individual purple bruises there by next weekend. He'll press on them when he spots them. Play a tune. Pretending each bruise is a black sharp or flat note on a keyboard.

'Like dough?' I say trying for humour.

'Like buns, *hun*,' he says with a quirk of his lips, and rolls me onto my back again to kiss me. I give in to the flutter and ripple of nerves he induces through my entire body and melt compliant below him into the mattress.

'Ow! Something keeps jagging me.' He shifts his weight so that his knee digs into the side of my thigh, and rummages through my duvet.

'The sequins keep falling off that cushion. Is it sequins?' I ask.

'Maybe.' He chucks the offending cushion across the room and drops his weight onto me again. Grinds his hips against mine. 'There, that's better— Ah! No, it's not! What *is* that?' He lurches off the bed. 'Get up, will you.'

I twist off the bed. Axel grabs the edge of my duvet and whips it away like a magician and then flicks it high into the air so that a tissue and hair-scrunchie disperse like fallen fruit. 'There! What's that?' He pushes a tumbled cushion out of the way and lifts the small black square plastic packet and holds it up so I can see the neon *GLIDE*.

'It's not mine!' I say.

'Whose is it then, Tavi?'

'I don't know. Douglas was chewing it.'

'Bullshit!' He thrusts the packet of lube in my face.

I look at it and see that it doesn't have a mark on it. Not a single telltale pug-tooth puncture. 'I . . .' I'm lost for words.

'Who have you had in here?'

'No one.'

'Don't lie to me! That's why you've been frigid. Because you're fucking someone else. Slut!'

'Axel! I haven't—'

'Don't believe you! It's Standish, isn't it? I've seen the way he looks at you.'

I'm incredulous that he thinks Olly Standish even knows who I am. 'No! It's not mine. Or anyone's . . .'

'It's someone's. And it's in *your* bed.'

'Douglas must've brought it in off the street.' My voice catches in my throat. My explanation sounds ridiculous.

But what else can I say? I don't know why it's here. No one's been in here. 'Maybe it's Milly's?'

'Milly's?' he says like I'm disgusting for even suggesting this of my little sister.

'She's almost sixteen! It might be hers.'

'Let's go ask her then!' he says, grabbing for my door handle. 'Milly!' he shouts. 'Come here, will you. We've got something to ask you!'

Milly calls up from the family room. 'Are we ordering pizza or not?'

I shout. 'Yeah . . . stay down there. Go ahead and order them on Mum's iPad! You know what I like!'

Axel glares at me, gripping the stairs newel post. 'What do you *like*, Octavia?' he says, and holds up the packet of lube, stretching the tip of his tongue out towards it, trying to lick it. 'You like that, don't you!'

'You're sick,' I say, and walk back into my room.

'Is Axel staying for pizza?' Milly shouts.

'No!' I half-heartedly shout back, but at the same time Axel replies, 'Yeah! Order me a meat feast!' He follows me inside and shuts my door. 'So when I'm not around whose meat have you been feasting on, Octavia?'

I sit on my bed and stare blankly at him. He knows I hate it when he calls me Octavia. But if I say anything he won't stop.

He slumps into my desk chair, looks at the square

of lube and then flicks it across the room at my face. I flinch and the sharp corner narrowly misses my eye, scratching my cheek instead. 'Ow! What the hell, Axel!'

'Now you know how I feel,' he mutters.

I say, 'How do you manage to twist everything so it's my fault?'

'Don't try and turn this on me!' Axel flares. 'I'm not the one who got caught lying about fucking other blokes. And after you made me feel guilty for not being able to— No wonder I couldn't! I could probably smell them on you. How many are there? How many guys are you having sex with that you need to lube up?'

I can't breathe. Can't get any air. I thought this was over. But he always manages to wind me back in and mess with my head.

'Aww, course you're gonna cry now!' He mimics me. *'I've never had sex before, Axel. No, I don't feel comfortable doing that . . . I'm all pure and sweet and innocent, Axel!'* His face drops. 'And all the while you've been with other guys, haven't you, Octavia! I must have MUG tattooed across my forehead.'

I really can't breathe. I grab at my shirt collar, the necklace there branding my skin, and pull it away from me. I'm taking in shallow gasps, but it feels like the universe has decided to crush me down into a tiny, irrelevant particle of non-existence. I choke out 'Can you go? I need you to leave, Axel . . .'

'I'm not leaving. We're having this out. You're always telling me you want to talk. So let's talk!'

'I can't. I don't . . .' I fold into useless, noiseless tears and the foetal position.

LISS

Ella Chat.

Ella: What about Good Vibes?

Ella: Vibe Tribe?

Ella: We Vibin?

Ella: Good Vibes Only. Vibe Revolution. Vibe Liberation Front. Feel the Vibe. Connect with the Vibe . . . Anything with Vibe?

Ella: Maybe using Vibe in the group name's too obvious. Could get messy at school. What do you think? I could send you a poll and you can get the others to vote? Or send me their numbers then I can ask them myself?

Me: Yeah, they all sound great.

Ella: Send me their numbers, will you?

I know the others won't want me giving their numbers to Ella, not without their permission, but how do I tell her that without hurting her?

Me: Probably best to ask everyone for numbers tomorrow when we meet. Some people are funny about privacy.

I press send quickly, close my phone, leave it on my bed and go downstairs to fix myself a smoothie.

And as the fruit swirls in the blender, I find myself thinking about Tavi. And Axel. I should have told her that

Axel asked me out on Monday morning. Should I? I don't know. I told Ella. Surely Ella will tell her if she thinks it's important. It's none of my business.

Tavi does seem unexpectedly nice. Why unexpected? Why am I surprised . . . ? I guess I've never had the chance to get to know her properly before now. And Axel's so dismissive. *Controlling and jealous* – that's how he described her. But she said Axel told her I'd said those horrible things about her. Who do I believe?

I should have asked him about the accusations on Monday. Spoken up. Like Ella manages so confidently. But I didn't, so . . . What would that achieve now? No point dredging up the past. Best to look forward.

TAVI

After a little while, Axel comes over and sits on the edge of my bed behind me. I don't know if it's the endorphins from crying or because I'm craving his hug, but my twisting confusion has turned into numbness. And when he pulls the duvet up off the floor and cocoons us under it. And spoons in behind me to hug me close. My breathing slows and I grip his arms like they're a lifebuoy, the only thing keeping me afloat out at sea.

'I'm sorry . . .' he whispers in my ear.

I nod. My tears are too close to the surface to speak.

He nuzzles in through my hair and kisses my ear.

'I don't know where it came from,' I say.

He squeezes me. 'Okay.'

'You have to trust me.'

'You know it's hard for me, with my dad and everything.'

'I know but *I* wasn't leaving you. *You* dumped *me*.' It feels easier to say this to him when I'm facing the wall.

'You're better off without me then!' he says loosening his hug. He sits up and releases me completely.

'Don't say that.' I twist and hug him round the waist. 'I miss you.' Fear that he gets up and walks out the door smothers my reluctance. 'Please . . .' I tug at his arms, for him to put them around me again.

He looks down at me. 'You don't need me,' he says. His face is flushed with that thick, sleepy haze he gets when he wants me.

I say quietly, 'I do.'

The doorbell rings again.

'Milly! Is that the pizzas?' I shout.

My phone rings. And it's Milly. I answer. 'Get the door,' I say.

'I'm in the loo. Can you get it?'

'Uh. Yeah. Pizzas are here!' I say to Axel, grabbing a sweatshirt and pulling it over my now-braless top half. I run downstairs. 'Coming!' The pizza boxes are sitting on the doorstep and the delivery girl's already climbing onto her moped. 'Thank you!' I shout and wave.

'Oh! Hello there!' shrills a familiar voice.

Aww, bollocks. Mrs Stanton's back. 'Hi!' I squat awkwardly to lift the pizzas, very aware I'm also missing my pants under my school skirt.

'I received a package for you! Just let me take my shopping inside and I'll pass it over the fence!'

'Eh, okay.' I pad tentatively barefoot across the grass and stand warming my fingers on the hot cardboard. Mrs Stanton unlocks her door. No beeping sound. Ella could've opened the back door after all. There's silence. No barking. I await a scream. Any noise to show that Petal hasn't eaten Douglas post coitus like a praying mantis. Then I hear, 'Oh? Where did I . . . ?' More silence. Then a single bark.

And Douglas jaunts out through Mrs Stanton's front door and jogs smartly up our path to sit on the front step. I leg it across the grass and let him inside.

'I, uhh?' I hear Mrs Stanton behind me.

'Yes?' I say.

'Did you . . . ?' She looks out to the road.

'You were getting my parcel.'

'The parcel . . . Um. Sorry, I was wrong. The parcel was for next door on the other side.'

Dishonest cow!

'Okay, well, thanks for your *help* then!' I open our front door and slide inside with the pizzas.

Axel's sitting on the stairs, cradling my dog to his bare chest like he's his baby. 'Don't know about you, Douglas,' he says, lifting him higher to kiss his exposed belly. 'But I think us men have worked up an appetite for pizza!'

CHAPTER 12

TAVI

'What's up?' Ella says next morning in the Upper Common Room.

'Mhm?'

'What's? Up?'

I shake my head at her distractedly. I should feel happy. I'm happy.

'Tavi, you've been sitting there like a zombie for the last ten minutes . . .'

'Hey, beautiful!' Axel says unexpectedly in my ear, making me flinch. His arm snakes round my neck and shoulders, pulling me back in my chair. And he kisses me on the temple.

I can't stop my eyes skittering over to Ella to see what she thinks.

'You're back together,' she says flatly, and pulls her bubble gum out from her mouth in a long strand, before winding it around her fingertip and chewing it again.

'Good to see you too, Gobby,' Axel says releasing me. He moves round the row of chairs to stand before me, blocking Ella out. 'Thought we could go to La Luna for lunch.'

'She can't,' Ella says, apparently untouched by Axel's casual use of the boys' disparaging nickname for her. 'She's helping me.'

Axel shifts towards Ella like he's going to start something.

'Yeah, let's go to La Luna,' I say quickly.

Ella chews her bubble gum with her mouth open, and then blows a big pink bubble until it pops and deflates. 'What goes up must come *down*,' she says. 'Ey, Axel?'

With a silent gasp, I hold my breath. She's remembered what I said!

Axel mutters something ending in *skank*. But his attention drifts and he heads across the common room towards Maz and Neil.

'What are you doing?' Ella says.

'Nothing,' I say, avoiding her eyes.

'You know he's no good for you!'

Larissa's approaching, so I don't reply. Has she told Larissa?

'You've been miserable for the last month,' Ella says. 'Longer!'

How does she know I've been miserable? Because I accidentally told her he couldn't get an erection? She's probably just pissed off I've ruined her matchmaking plans now we're back together. Which we're not. Not *definitely*. I haven't agreed to anything.

But there is something I do know – I've been lonely and miserable since me and Axel broke up on Friday night, so I'm starting to wonder whether it's better the devil I know . . .

But then, Larissa drops into the chair by Ella and looks between us, smiling. 'What happened with Douglas?' she asks.

It's such a pure smile that I find myself returning her mood with an actual grin, and replying, 'Douglas swaggered home bow-legged, ate pizza then passed out with exhaustion.'

She shakes her head, laughing, bouncing those long blonde waves. I can't stop staring at them. 'That was *too* funny yesterday,' she says. 'We should do it more often.'

'What? Dog burglary?' I say.

'Let's try cat burglary next time!' Larissa laughs. 'No, I mean the three of us hanging out.'

'Out of windows?' I say like a loser. But still I glance over my shoulder to check where Axel is before I agree. 'That would be cool!'

'She's back with Axel,' Ella says darkly.

They exchange a look. A look that I can't tell what the

hell they're thinking. What they're saying, silently. These two have their own secret language.

'We weren't really *split*,' I hear myself objecting, because no matter how nice Larissa is today and yesterday, she asked Axel out on Monday. And she and Ella want to split us up. And maybe because I have a chip on my shoulder about Larissa's looks. (She's basically a walking wet dream – long beautiful hair, longer legs.) Or because I'll never be Ella's *best* friend, I add, 'Axel just had to visit his gran – that's why he wasn't at my birthday.'

Larissa lifts her head in a slow-motion nod. 'Okay . . .'

I smile and lift my eyebrows at both her and Ella. *Who thinks I'm pathetic? I do!*

'I need to get to class,' Ella says with a weary sigh.

Larissa grabs her school bag. 'I'll chum you as far as the Science block, we need to talk about that *thing*.'

When they've gone, I look across the common room for Axel but he's already left.

LISS

'Quiet, please!' Ella snaps her fingers above her head.

I look nervously around my friends sitting in the dance-studio changing rooms. Irritation flicks across Ijeoma's lips as she closes her phone down. This was a mistake. I shouldn't have invited them.

'Welcome to our induction for *Buzz Club*!' Ella says brightly.

The low murmur grumbles to quiet. Most people are looking at Ella's Louis Vuitton weekender. Of course, she *had* to bring the vibrators in the LV.

'So, as I was saying, welcome to . . . BUZZ CLUB!'

No one says anything. Ella's ta-da reveal of the club's name – formulated after at least another twenty monologue messages at me last night – hasn't perhaps had the impact she expected. I shrink down inside my blazer and fiddle with the end of my ponytail.

'Anyway, although we're called Buzz Club,' she labours, 'I think this needs to be a secret club. So we should call it something else publicly, as a front.'

Ijeoma lets out a long sigh and leans back against the changing-room wall.

I want to weep.

'But, yeah, boring, I can work that out later.' Ella digs her hole deeper. 'And . . . I mean, *we* need a chairperson and I thought I could be . . . But if you'd rather nominate someone else, we can vote . . .'

No one objects. No one agrees either. I glance around the room – they're all avoiding Ella's eyes.

'I need to get my goalie pads before practice,' George

says. 'Can I just pick my vibrator now?' She points to the Louis Vuitton.

'We should've had more time in here,' Ella says. 'But that barre class—'

'That a yes?' George stands and holds her hand over the open bag, waiting to get the all-clear to dig in.

Suddenly remembering my offer for her to choose first, I say, 'Ijeoma was going to . . .' But Ijeoma shakes her head.

I settle back, wind my hair around my index finger.

'Give me a moment— I have a speech!' All blue skies and wide horizons, Ella says, 'With Buzz Club, it's my vision to start a revolution . . . ! A revolution to ensure that we females – female-identifying individuals – can own our own orgasms! No more will the source of our orgasms be at the hand – literally and metaphorically – of MALES!'

Ijeoma clears her throat.

Oh God . . .

'I have to go,' George says, her hand now grazing the bag's open zip.

'Look!' Ella snaps. 'Can't you just wait till I've finished?'

This is a disaster.

Eve says gently, 'I'll relay your vision to George, Ella. Ms White won't wait for her.'

'Great,' George says, dipping her hand into the bag and

pulling out a vibrator box. 'See you later, guys!' And she disappears out into the corridor.

A low murmur starts again. Ella catches my eye and beckons for me to come help her at the front. No danger. I give her a quick declining wave.

'Anyway.' Ella looks to her notes on her phone. 'I'm sure you've all got *lots* of ideas on how we can develop Buzz Club. Who we should invite to join. Formulate our mission statement . . .'

Ijeoma sucks through her teeth.

Ella eyes Ijeoma. 'But yeah, we should start with club member bonding. So you're all invited to Spíti Konstantinou this weekend for a sleepover!'

Confused looks are exchanged.

'My house,' Ella clarifies. 'Fully catered. My mum'll be there too. If you want to meet her?'

This generates reluctant interest from the others. We've all watched Kat Konstantinou's comedy series, even if the others wouldn't dream of admitting it to her daughter.

'I'll send you invites through a club group chat,' Ella says more confidently. 'Liss, you can give me their numbers!'

But her voice hangs in the air like an unpleasant smell. I know what they think of Ella. That she boasts about her situation. Famous mum. Fancy house. Plenty of money. I know they're here because I asked, quietly embarrassed, if anyone had an interest in joining a slightly *alternative* feminist club. One where they get a free vibrator.

But surprisingly, Eve was into the idea. And Ijeoma backed her up. The others followed.

I smile, trying to encourage positivity. 'That's okay, isn't it? Unless you want me to send out the invites? I suppose we'll need a club secretary, so I could handle that sort of thing?' I offer an easy, reassuring shrug to reinforce this isn't a big deal. That this will be fun!

Thankfully they make approving noises. Ijeoma's lips quirk in the hint of a smile.

I sit up and flick my ponytail behind me.

'Great. Brilliant!' Ella says, perking up. 'Okay, so who's next for the lucky dip?'

TAVI

Ella Chat.

> **Ella:** Sleepover. Mine. Tomorrow night.

'You sure you don't want us to come inside?' Mum says, eyeing Ella's mansion.

'I'll be alright,' I say, not feeling entirely alright.

'I don't know. Those girls look . . .' Mum and Mills turn in their seats to watch two girls from my year carry their sleeping and overnight bags up the steps and in through the pillared doorway. 'Actually, they look pretty cool – I'm not going to lie,' Mum says. 'Who are they?'

'They're in the First Eleven hockey team,' Milly explains. 'They're like, elite!'

'I didn't know they'd be coming too,' I say, hearing the apprehension in my voice.

'You okay?' Mum says.

'Yeah, course.'

'Okay then. Well, if you're not going to let us come in and look inside Kat Konstantinou's pad . . .' She pulls a doleful face.

'Bye.'

'O-kay then . . . Goodbye, Octavia. Enjoy hanging with the celebrity!' Mum reverses, pouts sadly at me, winks and they drive away.

I take a deep breath and throw my bag over my shoulder. This isn't what I was expecting when Ella said sleepover. I thought it would be her and me. Maybe with Larissa. But it looks like this is a full-on party, going by the mass of pink and red balloons and streamers framing the huge house's entrance porch and the two other cars dropping off girls when we arrived.

* * *

'The glitter's edible too, girls!' Ella's mum announces, dunking her chocolate-fountain-dipped strawberry into the bright-pink glitter. 'Your poos will literally sparkle all weekend!' she says, biting into her strawberry and swallowing.

The sporty girls (there's hockey and running squad here) laugh loudly, all six of them, and quickly dunk and stab their strawberries. I smile and suck my fingers. And wish Ella and Larissa would hurry up and come back down from Ella's room. They're setting up some sort of surprise for later.

'I have to go take a shower, girls – I've got a gig in Aberdeen tonight. Ella's granny will be over soon, so she's in charge while I'm away. Okay?'

The sporty squad nod and make impressed noises. We're all a bit starstruck by Ella's mum, and, personally, I'm worried I'll say something ridiculous in front of her and she'll put me in her comedy set. As for that freaky-sex-gadgets drawer that Ella mentioned, I'm not wondering where it is. Not at all – yeugh.

My phone vibrates with a new message, so I retreat to the kitchen windowseat and stroke Ella's cat while I read it. It's from Axel.

> **Axel:** I know you said you've got a family thing tonight but I was thinking of dropping in to yours . . .

Shit! I bite my thumbnail, wondering how to word my response.

> **Me:** Why don't we do something tomorrow instead?

> **Axel:** Could do, I guess.

> **Me:** Yay. That would be fun! Better go, I'm being called. See you tomorrow. xx

I quickly call Mum. 'Hey! No, everything's fine – can I ask you a favour though? If Axel turns up at home don't tell him I'm at Ella's house, okay? No, nothing's going on. It's just . . . Well, he's not that happy with Ella at the moment and— I know I did . . . We're seeing how it goes. Can you just tell him that I've gone to Granny and Grandpa's? Tell him you guys decided not to go after all. Yeah. It's no big deal. Okay, thanks. Bye!'

'The white lies we tell!' Eve Tennant – school's resident *'it girl'* – says, sitting down beside me on the windowseat.

I'm a little starstruck by Eve too. We've not spoken before.

'I told my mum we're organising a charity fundraiser,' Eve says. 'She'd never usually let me out for a sleepover the night before a hockey match. She's pretty strict.'

'Really? You always seem so . . . free.'

'Free?' Eve laughs. 'Thanks. I guess I'm good at hiding the reality!'

I bite my lip, mulling this unexpected revelation over. Ella said, Eve and Olly were having problems. *Crap sex.* Is it something like what's been happening with me and Axel? Or is it different? Was Axel telling the truth when he said Olly looks at me?

I guess I'm not the only one who's judged on outward appearances and hearsay. I feel bad that I've always just labelled Eve as a sporty – sexy – airhead. Ella's cat's purring and the other girls' chatter fills the silence between us.

ELLA

I pace round my room, waiting for Liss to come back from the loo. Go out onto the landing. Shut my door, pause, take a breath and open the door with a nonchalant swing and step inside. Scan the room as if it's the first time I'm seeing it. I straighten one of the face packs on my desk. At the nail bar, I move the nude Essie nail varnishes – *Clothing Optional, Master Plan, Topless & Barefoot,* and *Not*

Just a Pretty Face – to the back and arrange the brighter colour-pops – *Bikini So Teeny Baby*, *Tart Deco*, *Worth the Tassel*, *Fishnet Stockings* – to the front. Jesus, someone needs to overhaul the branding on this misogynistic shit! I should show Mum. She's bound to put this in her set. I open my make-up drawer, pick out one of the MAC lipsticks I stole from her and read the name on the bottom: *Men Love Mystery*. And another: *Daddy's Girl*. This is bullshit!

'Hey. Are you ready?' Liss says, finally appearing back from the loo.

'Yeah.' I slide the drawer shut and give the room one last check. 'You didn't just do a poo out there, did you?' I literally sprayed Mum's Le Labo perfume round the whole house before everyone arrived.

'Eh, no!' Liss blushes.

'Oh, for fuck's sake!' Now that lot'll tell people my house stinks of shit. I go out onto the landing and light a matching Le Labo candle.

'Shall we go down *now*?' Liss says.

I blurt, 'I've decided not to be chairperson!' There. I've said it now.

'Why? I'm not sure anyone else—'

'I'm going to be club secretary instead. You know, the mastermind behind the scenes. Missmind.'

'Right. Okay.'

'Yeah, so they won't think I'm taking charge anymore. I know they don't like me!'

'They like you . . .'

Try and sound convincing, Liss. 'You can be chairperson.'

Liss flushes.

'They want *you* in charge. You know that, don't you!'

She sighs, confirming she knows they fucking love her and they hate me. 'You're more suited to this sort of thing,' she says.

'Yeah. I am. But they all think I'm mouthy and gobby. So what can you do when you're surrounded by stupid! Maybe if you're the public face they won't mind if I run things in the background. And if you tell them that's the way it has to be, they'll accept it.'

'Please don't make me chairperson, Ella! I don't feel comfortable.'

'Someone has to be! Otherwise what's the point in having a club? We need purpose. We need direction.'

Liss just stares at me gormlessly, like a rabbit frozen in bright lights.

'Oh, for fuck's sake! Give me your phone.'

'Why?'

'Give me it. So I can tell everyone your plan.'

'My plan?'

'Yeah, *your* plan . . .' I stare at her.

Liss sighs and hands me her phone already open on the

Buzz Club private group. The one where she's the only admin. I type quickly, explain the plan, give instructions and, because I'm just a bit pissed off with them, add a couple of marginally amusing tweaks to the proceedings and press send to all of Buzz Club.

Liss holds her hand out. 'Can I have that back now?'

'Yeah, you can . . .'

She flicks her hand as if to say, *give me it then.*

'Why such a rush?'

'No rush.'

I narrow my eyes and look down as I quickly flick out of the app to see what else is open . . .

'Give me that!' Liss grabs her phone back. 'I'm going downstairs!'

CHAPTER 13

TAVI

By nine p.m. we've moved on from picking pink glitter and pizza toppings from between our teeth. Ella's granny is installed in the TV room with one of the biggest boxes of chocolates I've ever seen. And we're lying around Ella's bling bedroom in our pyjamas wearing spa treatment facemasks. We've been drinking a lethal concoction created by Ella mixing pink Prosecco, caramel vodka and raspberry Chambord liqueur. Pink Fluff – her cocktail – is sickly sweet and it's making me woozy.

'Right!' Ella says, clapping her hands. 'Face masks off! It's time to get down to business.'

The other girls, some a little drunk, some sober – dependent on their dedication to the hockey match tomorrow – splinter off between Ella's en suite and the family bathroom out on the landing. I wander into the en suite and wait to wash my face with cold water to try and wake myself up. I'm not really sure what business we're getting down to.

Once we've all returned, pink faced and squeaky clean, Ella locks her door. Larissa drags Ella's wicker chair – an elaborate thing with a high back, shaped like a fanned-out peacock tail – to the end of Ella's bed. Ella arranges cushions and pillows on the floor around the chair. Most of us stand around like spare parts waiting to be told what to do, until Ella waves for us to sit on the cushions.

Then she dives into her walk-in wardrobe and emerges carrying the silky Wonder Woman cape she wore last year for Halloween and lays it out on the end of her bed. Next, she grabs the silver *Frozen* tiara and wand from her bookcase and sets them beside the cape, and finally she adds the bottle of Chambord.

Instead of sitting in the peacock chair, Ella goes to her bedside cabinet and removes a pink sparkly notebook. She opens it near the front and walks back to the chair, reading aloud: 'I call to order the second meeting of the secret club, now publicly referred to as Book Club.'

Oh, Book Club!

She continues, 'Here are the minutes from our inaugural meeting,' she tips the notebook forward displaying her messy handwriting, 'should any member wish to review them. The proposed agenda for the next meeting will also be voted for and documented here – in what shall be known as our club femual . . .'

Femual?

'Let it be noted that we welcome one new member tonight.'

I smile, because obviously that's me. I didn't know Ella ran a secret book club. I like books. I'm definitely in.

'Welcome to Book Club, Khair.'

Ehh?

'Thanks,' Khair says beaming. 'I'm excited to join!'

'Plenty more *excitement* to come,' Ella says scrunching her nose. 'I'm sure you'll find our club *stimulating* in every sense . . .'

No one laughs. But Ella acts like they did. 'So, to the first item on our agenda. We need to crown our chairperson, our leader. Here's the chair—' Ella gestures to her wicker chair, signalling for us all to make admiring noises. She gets a few grunts. Then she says, 'Sit in your chair, Tavi.'

You know when you think you've heard wrong so you sit waiting for something to happen. But then you realise everyone's sort of, quietly, laughing at you because they know something you don't. And, yes, Ella did say sit in the chair. But because of the smirk on their faces, you don't move. And you feel sick. You know that feeling?

'Tavi, we've got a lot to get through tonight. I have an agenda. Just sit in the chair.'

I stand and ease myself suspiciously into the chair.

'Right . . .' Ella moves behind me so I can't see what she's doing, then she reappears and continues, 'as nominated by your fellow founding members – me and Larissa,' she puts the cape over my shoulders and fastens it at my neck, 'at a very recent strategic meeting,' tiara goes on my head, wand in my right hand, 'and in lieu of your previous absence,' bottle of Chambord in left hand – oh now I get it, it looks like one of those royal orbs – 'we . . .' Ella disappears behind me again.

I try to turn to see what she's doing, but Larissa snaps, 'Ah!' wagging her finger for me not to look.

'. . . now crown you . . .' Ella says from just over my shoulder, 'Chairperson of Buzz Club, and Leader of our Revolution!' And she places a cushion on my lap.

Everyone bursts into applause.

With my hands full of regalia, I look down at my lap. Sitting atop a purple velvet cushion is my purple silicone vibrator.

Shock makes me think I'm seeing things, so I don't immediately react. Not until Ella's words finally sift through my brain cells. *Chairperson. Buzz Club? Leader. Revolution . . . ?*

I blurt, 'I said no revolution! NO revolution!'

'Shh!' Ella hisses, looking towards her bedroom door.

'Why am I leader of *your* revolution? You started all this!'

'Well, technically you started it because you were the one who gave me the idea of giving you a vibrator when Axel dumped you! I thought you'd want to be part of this?' Ella gestures to the seven other girls around me. And I realise what she's blatantly saying is *you have no other friends, Tavi. Here, I've found you some friends. Friends who are packing their own personal benefits, just like you!*

And suddenly everyone pulls out a vibrator. From hoodies, pyjama pockets, cleavages and below cushions. A rainbow of all shapes and sizes. And with a quick twiddle or button scroll these personal benefits start buzzing.

Ella's the last and, sure enough, pulls out an ombré vibrator from the waistband of her sleep-shorts, drops down onto a cushion and with a flourish starts hers buzzing before reaching out towards my feet.

I tuck them back out of her reach.

A few others join in and, with an out-of-synch accompaniment to the frenetic buzzing, chant together, 'We praise you, our *Leader* . . . for showing us the way to own our orgasms . . .' like they've rehearsed it in advance. Then they wave their arms exultantly in the air, vibrators aloft. 'We bow to your superior technology.' And bow flat to the ground.

This is hell! A ridiculous hell. I'm tempted to bowl the bottle of Chambord at Ella's head, but I think better of it, dump the *Frozen* wand and open the bottle to take a swig. *Yeegh*.

'Have more Pink Fluff, Tavi,' Ella says, getting up quickly. 'Everyone. Plenty more where that came from.'

I drink a couple of gulps of the sugary froth, which is a bad idea because I'm not great with booze at the best of times and this is not one of those better times. I sit back in the chair and breathe carefully through my thundering heart.

The others get more comfortable on their cushions, waggling their devices about in the air along with their plastic champagne flutes, like they're perfectly partnered accessories.

I try to ignore the cushion on my lap and its cherry-on-top. Wait, how did she get it here? 'Did you steal this from below my bed?' I say.

'Might've. Now, down to business! Maybe turn those off for a bit,' Ella says, stopping her own vibrator. 'Tavi, as you've probably grasped, this is Buzz Club. Our secret society where we plot revolution and we meet to discuss our vibrators.'

'I haven't agreed to join,' I say stubbornly.

'You started it,' Ella says. 'We've joined you.'

'I didn't.'

'You did. You're leading, we're following, remember. Anyway, I have to get through this agenda before my gran comes upstairs so will you let me get on?'

I sigh because I'm not speaking to Ella anymore. Buzz Club . . .

'As I said, Buzz Club is a secret club – publicly known as Book Club. We're invite-only and all new members need to be approved by two existing members.'

I widen my eyes at Ella. What does she mean *new* members?

Ignoring me, she continues, 'So the second item on the agenda, post crowning-of-our-Leader is . . .' Ella runs her finger down her notebook page, while she waggles her vibrator in her other hand like it's a biro and she's bored in Double History. 'Rules of Buzz Club! The first rule of Buzz Club is . . .'

I drain the last drop of my Pink Fluff and say, 'There is no Buzz Club?'

'No, I looked this up. It's – you do not talk about Buzz Club!'

'So we're not talking about it,' I say. 'Fine by me. Great first rule.'

'What do you mean, you looked it up?' Eve says. 'Are there other Buzz Clubs in the world? Is it a thing?'

'No, I don't think so,' Ella says. 'Maybe . . . Check that, someone.'

'What's the second rule?' I say. I'm impatient to get this over with so I can get this thing off my knee.

Ella looks at the back of her notebook. 'DO NOT TALK about Fight Club!'

'Buzz Club,' Larissa says.

'Yeah . . .'

'You said, Fight Club.'

'I mean Buzz Club.'

'That's the same as the first rule,' I say.

'I know that, but that's what it says online. The repetition reinforces the importance of the first rule.'

'I thought you said Buzz Club wasn't already a thing?' Eve says. 'What are you looking up?'

'She's quoting a film called *Fight Club*,' George Marston says, sounding bored.

I can't rip my eyes from George. She's poking her rubber willy into her ear as she reads her phone.

Ijeoma Adams says, 'Those are ridiculous rules. Fair enough if we were in a chest-beating misogynistic fight film but how can we invite new members if we can't actually talk about this? How are we allowed to even have this meeting now – we're talking about it!'

'Fine then!' Ella says, slapping her pink notebook closed. 'What do you suggest?'

Eve says, 'Rule One should be that we can't speak to anyone outside the society about this, unless we're inviting them in and only then if we have two members' approval?' She looks at me like I make the decisions around here.

I shrug in agreement.

'And Rule Two,' Eve continues, 'should really be about hygiene because I'm not going to my family doctor because I've developed a UTI. My mum will know Olly and me have been shagging.'

I look at my vibrator with renewed fear. Can they cause UTIs? Not that I can totally remember which one's a UTI. Urinary something-beginning-with-T Infection.

'Rule Three should be no boyfriends,' Ella says. She glances at Ijeoma and adds, 'Or girlfriends. This is a singles club.'

'Why?' says Ijeoma, looking ready to walk out the door.

'Because it should be us empowering ourselves. Getting to know our bodies. Being an island, at one with our orgasms.'

'And we can't do that in a relationship?' Eve says.

'What about Maz?' Ijeoma says.

Ella shrugs. 'I'll dump Maz tomorrow.'

'Tavi?' Eve says. 'You're the leader. Do we have to be single?'

'No,' I say decisively.

'Oh yeah, how could I forget, you're back with Axel,' Ella mutters.

'Wait! Didn't you just say Axel dumped her?'

'But now you're back together?'

I glare at Ella. 'No. I mean— Yes, we're together. He just went to his gran's.'

'Rechargeable batteries, that should be the third rule,' George says.

'Does yours take batteries? Mine plugs in.'

'Yeah, mine plugs in too.' Everyone murmurs in agreement, much to George's disgust and my relief that they're no longer fixating on Axel and me.

'You lot need to buy me rechargeable batteries then!' George says. 'It's not fair if I have to keep buying batteries and you can all plug yours in.'

'Yeah, yeah. We'll chip in and get you them,' Ella drawls. 'But that was a lucky dip in the changing rooms. And you were in such a rush to go first so you can't blame anyone else.'

George scowls at Ella.

'What do you mean, the changing rooms?' I say.

Eve answers, 'We had our first meeting there yesterday – when we got to pick out our vibrators.'

I grimace, imagining all those boxed vibrators in school. If mine had been there and I'd been caught with it, would the teachers know what it was? Mum hasn't said anything to me about Ella's present. So she hasn't cottoned on . . . ?

I notice my vibrator has a tiny hole at one end, which I guess is where the cable I saw in the neoprene case plugs. So no batteries needed for mine either. 'Where's the case for this, Ella?' I say suddenly.

'Left it under your bed so you wouldn't realise I'd pinched it. I knew you wouldn't use it!'

'Haven't you used it?' Eve says.

'No,' I admit.

Everyone looks disappointed in me.

'You're right,' I say slyly. 'I should stand down as leader. I'm sure Ella has much more miles on hers already. Let *her* be leader.'

'Nice try, Tavi,' Ella drawls. 'It's your choice if you use it or not. If you don't then you can be the Virgin Mary of Buzz Club. If you do, you can be Mary Magdalene. Either way you're Mary.'

'Ella,' I say, 'I have no idea what the fuck you're talking about.'

'I haven't either,' Ijeoma mutters.

George interjects, 'I've just looked up the third rule of Fight Club!'

'Don't talk about Fight Club?'

'Nup. Third rule of Fight Club – someone yells stop, goes limp, taps out, the fight is over . . .' George lifts her eyebrows suggestively.

Everyone bursts out laughing.

Ella says, 'That can *definitely* be the third rule of Buzz Club!'

* * *

Mum's driving me home in the morning, thankfully giving me peace to be mute and groggy. When a message from Axel breaks my Zen.

Axel Chat.

> **Axel:** What time are you back from your grandparents'? Caroline and David said I can take you to the cinema.

'Why didn't you tell me you spoke to Axel? You told him he can take me to the cinema?'

'We didn't say that – we said it was up to you!' Mum protests, turning into our street. 'Didn't he ask you?'

'Yeah. He did . . .' He didn't. 'I was just . . . doesn't matter,' I mutter.

'What's going on between you and Axel anyway? First he misses your party, then you're split up and now you're *seeing how it goes.* What's next?'

'Why do you always have to put a label on things?' I say.

'I don't have to put a label . . .'

'Don't you? Okay . . . !' I say, sounding totally thrawn and passive aggressive.

We pull onto our driveway.

Mum unclips her seatbelt but doesn't get out. 'Tavi, what's going on?'

'Nothing! I'm just tired . . .' I trail off when I realise that Axel's leaning against our front door frame chatting to Milly, who's sitting on the front step. 'Mum, Axel's already here . . .'

She cranks round to look at him but doesn't wave like usual. 'Do you want me to tell him that you *can't* go to the cinema . . . ? What do you want me to do?'

I'm not sure why Mum's saying it like that! I say, 'I'll go to the cinema.'

CHAPTER 14

LISS

Book Club Chat.

> Group Admin Ella Konstantinou has changed this group's name from Buzz Club to Book Club

> **Ella:** As Liss has decided to hand the role of club secretary over to me, here are our agreed rules.

Ella PDF:

BOOK CLUB RULES

1) You do not talk about *Book Club*. (To anyone outside Book Club, unless another member agrees in advance. You can then – discreetly – sound that person out on how open-minded they are towards *books* and *reading* in general. Only when you're sure they might be receptive to *book* ownership can you invite them to *Book Club*.)
2) Health & Safety – keep your *books* and *pages* clean!
3) Someone yells stop, goes limp, taps out, it's THE END . . . (See Rule 5 iii.)
4) Individual *reading* experiences may remain your own business. However, open discussion on how a *book* specifically *moved* you is welcomed and encouraged.
5) *Book Club* is here to aid in the *reader* experience. Proposed items for discussion:

   i. Environment – secret archiving ideas for book storage; securing the privacy of your *reading* room whilst *reading*; ensuring silence beyond your *library* . . .

> ii. Innovation in the *Book* Industry – presentations on new *books*, tech etc.,
> iii. Narrative Arc: prologue to epilogue & ensuring you reach the *story*'s climax,
> iv. Genre Preferences: commercial to experimental fiction and everything literary between. What's your *Fantasy Fiction?*
> v. Debate on *Books* v *Personal Improvised Poetry* . . .
>
> 6) When progressing from solo reading to reading in pairs or groups – see Rule 2 – book jackets are essential!

The five of us from hockey who were at Ella's last night have congregated at the back of the team minibus – we're heading to our away match in Perth.

Among us, however, are two *outsiders* who weren't there. We've done well and not mentioned Buzz Club but they've been asking about the sleepover and now the Book Club Rules have just come through on our phones, and we're in hysterics (kudos to Ella, she must've worked hard on putting that together). So now I can see George is literally twitching under the struggle to stay subtle and not reveal all.

Sure enough, she says, 'Come on! Can we just invite them already?'

Ijeoma's sitting beyond George, by the window. She

shrugs and looks over my way. I feel that cramp of excitement, and smile as if to say, *I don't mind.*

'Go on then,' Ijeoma says.

George blurts, 'You guys want a vibrator?'

Ijeoma covers her smirk with her hand.

'Urgh?' Gemma Christie says, scrunching her nose.

'I mean, like a new one,' George adds. 'Not a Vinted one. I'm no good at this—! Ijeoma, tell them about the revolution stuff!'

'Oh, you mean the pink-glitter chocolate strawberries,' Ijeoma says. 'Or do you mean the pink-and-red balloon-streamer monstrosity, shaped like a giant vulva?'

She clocked that then . . . No one else appeared to recognise Ella's special-order rubber creation above her front door.

'Or the Pink Fluff cocktails,' Ijeoma continues, 'spa treatments and girly sleepovers . . . Yeah, we're definitely breaking down stereotypes with our Barbiecore revolution.' Ijeoma flicks her eyebrows at me as if to say, *am I right?*

I briefly smile, but I'm not with her on this one. Ella's trying to do something, and she put a lot of thought and effort into last night so that everyone would enjoy themselves.

'That sounds fun!' Gemma says.

Eve pipes up, 'It was! And, Ijeoma, you ate so many of those strawberries, your pre-match poo will literally sparkle – Barbie pink!'

We laugh.

Ijeoma does too.

Even though we may have found two new members for Buzz Club, I can't help but worry that this friction between Ijeoma and Ella is going to have me conflicted.

TAVI

In the front seat on the top deck of the number 28 bus, staring straight ahead, Axel says, 'Have a nice time at your grandparents' . . . ?'

'Eh, yeah. It was good.'

He doesn't react again, doesn't even move, until the next stop. When he finally looks me up and down, lifts a lock of my hair and tucks it behind my ear. 'Your hair's a mess.'

'Oh!' I pull my pony out and slick everything back tight.

He watches me. 'That's better,' he says.

I smile awkwardly.

He says, 'So what did you do at your grandparents'?'

'Uh . . . I helped Gran make a cake. And we watched TV.'

'Oh, yeah? What did you watch?'

'Just . . . I dunno. *EastEnders?*' Gran watches that, I think . . . Is it still on TV?

'Uh-huh?'

'Are we not getting off for the Odeon?' I say confused, when we pull up at the cinema stop and Axel doesn't move or let me up.

He shrugs like he doesn't care anymore and stares ahead again.

'Are we going to Cineworld?'

Axel shrugs again.

We sit in silence until we're almost in town. 'What about you?' I say. 'Get up to much last night?'

'Yeah.'

'Yeah? What?'

'Neil met this girl off Tinder, she had friends.' He shrugs. 'We hung out in Dawson Park.'

Suddenly, my chest's ice.

Axel turns to look at me with lazy eyes. 'Hurts, doesn't it,' he says.

I stare at him.

'You were at Ella's. With *Larissa*! Eve posted a video of you eating chocolate marshmallows. Milly just confirmed it.'

Tucking my arms round my waist, I say, 'It was Book Club . . .'

'Book Club? Since when are you into books?'

'Eh, since always . . .'

'Bullshit!'

I blink furiously trying to stop my tears.

'I thought you wanted us?'

'I do,' I manage.

'No, you don't—!' He kicks the bus seat in front. 'Larissa's trying to break us up! Ella too. You know that!'

I grip my fists tight, biting my tongue. Are they trying to break us up? Why's he making such a big thing of this? Why can't I hang out with them?

He shifts and I flinch. But he leans to press the STOP button and swings out of his seat and down the staircase. I'm expected to follow. I'm *very* tempted to stay put.

But I do follow, and step off into the rain. Axel pulls up his hood. My jacket doesn't have a hood. He's ignoring me. Choosing, instead, to sneer at the statue of Queen Victoria across the road. And with a grunt, mutters, 'Fat bint.'

It feels like he's directing the insult at me, though, for yesterday, for hanging out with the girls. Because Victoria's sitting on her throne. Crown on her head. Sceptre and orb in her hands. She's even got her bronze Wonder Woman-style cape over her shoulders.

'Right!' I say, daring to channel super woman strength. 'I thought we were seeing a film so I'm going to DCA.' I pull my collar up and set off for Reform Street.

'Wait. I was going to the Odeon!' Axel shouts after me.

I swing round. 'So why didn't you get off the bus earlier?' He shrugs and pouts stubbornly.

I know why. Because he's punishing me. I disobey. Go

to my friend's house. Hang out with his ex . . . So I get punished. I say, 'I'm not doing this anymore!'

'Fine, we'll go to DCA – it's always showing poncy art-student shite but if that's going to make you happy!'

'Yeah, it is actually,' I say, folding my arms.

'At least one of us is happy then . . .' he mutters, walking past me.

In the cinema, we buy our tickets separately, and drinks and snacks – not without Axel raising his eyebrows at my chocolate. 'I'm just popping to the loo,' I say, before we head to the film. 'Will you wait for me?'

'Yeah,' Axel says. But when I try to hand him my drink, he adds, 'I'll wait inside.' And he walks away to the screen.

The movie experience is just as bad. It's like a tense first date. Where you're totally conscious of the other person's arm and body. But instead of a will-we-won't-we-kiss vibe, I can feel his hostility rolling off his elbow.

ELLA

'We could get sushi? You like chicken katsu,' I suggest to Yaya for Saturday lunch.

'And those gyoza things, I like them,' she says.

'Great.'

Mum appears yawning, dressed in leggings and a big slouchy sweatshirt with her hair, and glasses, piled up on her head.

'We're thinking sushi,' I say.

'Sounds good,' Mum says looking in the fridge. She emerges with a sugar-free Red Bull, cracks it open and gulps it.

'How was last night?' Yaya asks.

'It *was*!' Mum says, clunking the can onto the marble worktop.

'Oh.'

'We were thinking of going for sushi now,' I say.

'Going?' Mum whines. 'Can't we get a delivery? I don't want to go out among the humans again before tonight's gig!'

I look at Yaya.

She turns to Mum. 'Go get smartened up, Katerina. You've not taken your daughter out anywhere for weeks!'

Mum screws up her nose, downs the rest of her can of Red Bull, chucks it in the recycling and walks out of the kitchen with her shoulders slumped like she's a little kid who's been told off by her mum. Which she has. Then suddenly she's back in the doorway. 'I really need to prep for tonight,' she says. 'Just for an hour. If we get takeaway then I can do that now while we're waiting for the delivery, then once the food arrives, I'm all yours.'

'Until you have to go out among the humans again,' I say coolly. 'Liss and Maz's parents actually parent, you know. They go watch their matches—'

'You don't play sport.'

'They're always out doing things together at weekends. Family stuff!'

'Well, lucky Liss and Maz's *parents* that they work on a weekday or at least *one of them* has their weekends free to do all that fun family stuff. My job doesn't work like that, hun. And sorry I'm all you've got, but I think I'm not doing *too* badly managing to provide you with all *this* on my own! Funding lavish sleepovers. Cleaners coming in to make the place pristine afterwards, so you don't have to lift a finger! I'm—'

'That was your choice, Katerina,' Yaya says firmly. 'You chose to have Eleanora alone. Eleanora didn't choose all this.' Yaya gestures to the kitchen. 'You did.'

'Don't *you* start!'

Well said, Yaya! I mean, I probably would've chosen this kitchen, to be fair. Mum's got great taste. Apart from this table. The squeaky white lacquer gives me the ick.

But I refrain, because now Yaya's picked the scab off the emotional wound I usually keep hidden below a plaster of *I don't even care*. I'm not feeling that hungry for sushi now.

'Fine!' Mum strops. 'I'll go get dressed up and we'll all go have sushi like a happy family!'

I let out a massive sigh, and shout after her, 'Don't bother! I don't want to go out anymore . . . !'

Mum comes back to the door. 'You sure?'

'I'm choosing the whole food order,' I say, not making eye contact. 'You'll have to eat whatever I get!' I'm warming up now. '*And* you'll let me film us eating for my channel because *that lot* last night refused to film any mukbang or ASMR. I can't believe we had a chocolate fountain and all those balloons and glitter and fruit, and I got zero footage. And yeah, thanks *very much* to your cleaning crew for clearing everything away so I couldn't even film myself after they'd all gone. Who gave them the right to pop those balloons?'

Mum doesn't even acknowledge my outburst, and just says, 'Tomorrow morning . . .'

Her exaggerated pause means I have to look at her.

She continues, 'I need a quick inspiration trip round the V&A for the new set. But we can go on a family outing afterwards . . . ?'

'Maybe,' I say, and open my phone to start choosing our food. 'If the food arrives earlier, you'll have to stop earlier!'

'Okay. Thanks, boss.'

I don't smile. And I don't tell her that I have an idea for her new set. If she appears for lunch. And actually listens to me for a change . . . I might tell her about it then.

I guess I can fill you in on the lack of a second-parent

thing... Obviously I do have a genetic dad! It's not like I was created of immaculate conception. I'm not *that* special. But that is the beginning, and the end, of my creation story. *The man dideth deposit his genetics. End of.* Aka Mum used a sperm donor.

All I know – until I get access to his name and stuff when I'm eighteen – is he was twenty-three when he donated (ten years younger than Mum when she had me), six foot two, dark hair, green eyes, worked as a bricklayer and part-time model and liked to go to the gym. The message he wrote on the clinic paperwork for me just says, Hope you have a good life, kid. Stand up for yourself. Work hard at school. Don't sweat the big stuff.

I only noticed this year that he got the saying wrong. Should be Don't sweat the small stuff. Which makes me hope I take after Mum in the intelligence stakes. Because I sure don't take after him in the physical, apart from the green eyes. And the dark hair, but Mum's dark too. I did wonder if maybe he was really laid back and just didn't want me to stress about anything, no matter the size...

Anyway, I've got Yaya.

She's my granny and second parent in one. What more do I need or expect to achieve from making contact with my genetic dad? He donated to help *someone else* become a parent. Not because he wanted to be my parent himself.

So, I'm fine.

As long as I don't peel the plaster back, pick the scab off and have a little look at that festering wound below. That void.

Yaya says, 'Are you sure you don't want to go into town, Eleanora?'

'It's fine,' I say.

'Look at these.' I spill an armful of nail varnishes and make-up – a mix of both mine and Mum's – onto the glossy kitchen table. We've finished lunch and Yaya's gone upstairs for a snooze.

Mum lifts her Red Bull can. 'I've just had my gels done. You're not touching my nails.'

'That's not what this is,' I say, setting the bottles upright.

'What is it then?'

'Here. See this Opi Nail Lacquer? What colour would you call it?'

'Taupe.'

'It sure is. Guess what they've called it.'

'Terrible taupe? Mushroom? Shitake? Bloody boring beige?'

'No. None of those. It's called . . . you ready?'

'Eh, yeah.'

'It's called *Taupe* . . . I pause for effect, '*-less Beach*.'

'Taupe-less Beach?'

'Yup.'

'That's kind of funny.'

'You don't think it's misogynistic?'

'Well, yeah. What's your point?'

'What about this? Very pale pink?'

She stares at the nail varnish. 'Are we going with a theme here?'

'We're going with a theme. Say what you see.'

'It looks like . . .' She scrunches her nose up in disgust. 'It looks like those packs of anaemic raw sausages you get in Morrisons, the ones with no skin. You know—'

'Shut up!'

'What? It's not called Scottish skinless sausage?'

'Close enough – *My Very First Knockwurst*.'

'You're lying!' She grabs the nail varnish from me and holds it at arm's length to read the bottom because she doesn't have her reading glasses. 'What the hell?' she says once she's focused. 'Give me those!' She grabs up another nude. '*Pale to the Chief* . . . ? Fucking hell, Ella! This is some racist shit, not just misogynistic.' She lifts a bright-red varnish that I took from her room. '*I'm Not Really a Waitress*? That one's weird. But also— Who the hell's coming up with these? Don Draper from *Mad Men*?' She looks at another red as she takes an excited gulp of her Red Bull and full-on chokes. I have to wallop her on the back. She's still laughing and spluttering when she hands me the varnish bottom-side up: *A Little Guilt Under the Kilt.*

I'm rifling in the back of my chest of drawers for any more dodgy make-up names I've missed, when I hear a tap on my bedroom window.

'What do you want?' I say, opening the window to Maz who's standing on the TV room's flat roof.

'You told me to come over.'

'Yeah, well, you can't stay,' I say as he proceeds to climb inside. 'Mum's still here and we're working on something important together.'

'Can't I just wait up here and then we can hang out when she leaves?' He reaches out to give me a hug and I dodge him.

'No. Bog off.'

'Why are you being so mean . . . ?' Maz pushes out his bottom lip like he's about to start crying.

'Because I'm a mean girl! And I have revolutionary work to do that's going to change the world. Or at least the name of a lipstick if I'm lucky. Bye.' I peck him on the lips and push him back to the window.

CHAPTER 15

LISS

Book Club Chat.

> **Ella:** Happy Sunday, Book Clubbers! Hope you've had a 'stimulating' weekend thus far! Just a reminder to bring your 'books' with you tomorrow night.

Ella PDF:

> AGENDA FOR NEXT BOOK CLUB, MONDAY 27th JAN
> VENUE: Tavi's house, straight after school.
> Show-and-tell – Tavi to present to group on what she loves about her *book*, and everyone else to follow with what they love about theirs.

I'm surprised Tavi agreed to have Buzz Club at her house – considering her ruined birthday party and the dog burglary debacle... And for her to lead the meeting? She's braver than me!

Is she though... Tell me Ella hasn't gone ahead and invited everyone without even asking Tavi!

Another message pops up, distracting me.

Hockey Chat.

> **Ijeoma:** Who's on for a spa? My muscles are solid after yesterday's match.

> **George:** Can't. Being dragged to watch wee bro's Sunday mini-touch-rugby.

> **Eve:** Yes! Need a jacuzzi. Should never have drunk that pink stuff Friday night.

> **George:** You can't still be hungover!

Eve: Probably not but everything hurts worse than usual. Help me!

Ijeoma: Jacuzzi and plunge then!

Me: Poor you, Eve. Ijeoma's right. Hot and cold will help. I need it too. What time?

When I arrive at the gym, Ijeoma's waiting in the café with a couple of our other teammates. She's wearing my favourite black Nike zip top again. 'Hey!' I say. 'Eve not here yet?'

She waves her phone at me. 'She'll be here in ten.'

'Shall we wait?'

'Nah, she'll find us in the spa.'

'Okay. Cool.' I follow Ijeoma and the others through the swing doors. She turns and smiles at me. I smile back. We walk together in silence, as the others chat. 'I'm just popping to the loo,' I say, once we're inside the female changing rooms.

'See you in the spa then,' Ijeoma calls after me.

'Yeah!' I answer brightly. I lock the loo door and drop

my bag on the floor. Shut the loo seat and sit on it. I don't even need the toilet. I fold my arms, jiggle my head and exhale. I'd better not wait here long – she'll think I'm doing a poo. I suppose she might think I've got my period. I should go back out. But if I see her changing! My whole body flushes. And I have to press on my chest to try and calm my drumming heart.

I'll stay here a bit longer. I look at my Apple Watch, and the seconds flick through a whole minute. Then I do a nervous pee. Take a while washing my hands and using the dryer. When I emerge at the lockers, I see Ijeoma and the others – changed into their costumes – heading through to the pool shower. She waves to me. I wave back.

I'm sitting clutching my towel around me, psyching myself up, when Eve appears.

'Morning! Is it still? Ugh, it's already midday. I need this so bad! Have the others gone in?'

'Uh. Yeah, they've just—'

'Don't wait for me. I've already got my bikini on. I won't be long.'

'No, it's alright. I'll wait.' I can't walk out there on my own anyway.

'Aww, thanks. I couldn't find my one piece,' she says,

stripping off her sweatshirt and tracksuit bottoms. 'So bikini it is!'

'Oh! I'm wearing a—'

'Is that a bikini too? Oh, I don't feel so bad then. You know what that lot are like! They'll probably take the piss, but we can be bikini babes together.'

I grip the towel. Why didn't I bring a one piece? Shit. Why did I wear this?

'Coming?' Eve says.

'Yeah,' I say weakly, following her. Still holding my towel tight.

'You'd better shower,' she says. 'You know what the lifeguards are like.'

'Course.' I hang my towel on the hook and quickly soak myself.

'Nice bikini! Where's it from? I had one like that a few years ago but the spots were more peachy pink.'

'It's ASOS.'

'Love a bit of ASOS!'

As I follow Eve into the spa area, I hold my towel to my front, pretending to dry my face, but then she hangs hers on a hook and I have to do the same. Someone wolf-whistles from the jacuzzi. 'Yaass, queens! Work it!' And Eve catwalks, boofing her newly short hair, overdramatically swinging her hips and spins, before sashaying down the steps. I'm blushing all over again and scurry after her, quickly submerging into the jacuzzi without making eye contact with anyone. Under, I push through the water and sink onto the tiled bench by Eve. This is getting out of hand. I need to pull myself together. Can they see I'm acting differently? Do they know? My eyes skirt around the group, checking whether anyone's watching me. And meet Ijeoma's eyes.

After about five minutes, Eve says, 'I don't care what Ms White says, I'm going in the sauna.'

I'm lying back with my head against the wall and my eyes closed. But I'm listening to everything. Totally aware of where people are. Thankful that I can now blame my blushes on the hot water.

'It'll make you more dehydrated,' I hear Ijeoma say, and my stomach flips.

'Liss? You want to come to the sauna?'

'I'm okay here, thanks,' I say.

'The jet timer will go off in a few minutes . . .' Eve says.

'I might go for a swim then,' I offer, without opening my eyes.

'Okay, give us a wave when you do.'

I feel Eve move away from my side and hear the other girls agree to go with her to the sauna. I try to sense a movement in the water, to judge how many people are leaving the jacuzzi. And then I feel someone move alongside me.

'It's going to make her feel worse,' Ijeoma says.

I sit up and stare after Eve and the others padding up the steps, going to rinse off under the rain-shower. I say, not looking at Ijeoma, 'I don't know how she played so well yesterday with a hangover.'

'She's a highly tuned machine. And she needed to let loose on Friday.'

'Because of Olly?' I ask, now looking at Ijeoma.

'Yeah . . .' Ijeoma stretches and flexes out her shoulders before checking her long braids are secured on the top of her head.

I try not to imagine touching her bare skin. But I can almost feel the slick of its surface under my fingertips. The thrill in my groin as I picture tracing down the fall of her neck, onto her shoulder. Up over the curve of her deltoid muscle. Down her arm. I need the ice plunge! Only . . . I can't move. I quickly look to Eve and the others just as they close the door of the sauna behind them. And the release, the momentary relief of not being watched. Being alone with her. I let out a groan . . .

Ijeoma reacts. She turns in surprise. Our eyes collide. Like there's no one else here. I'm breathless. Lips part, trying to hide that my heart and lungs are thundering for oxygen, thundering for her to touch me. Kiss me. I've imagined it every night for the last month. When I use my vibrator, I think of her. I want her.

Her face smooths and she sighs. With? Relief? Does she know? Does she—? And something I only dreamt of this morning happens – her fingers find mine underwater, and intwine.

TAVI

Sunday teatime, Mum goes to the takeaway to collect our family Thai banquet for four, even though it's just us three eating – Dad's gone to the pub. Milly and me impatiently flick through our phones until we can un-pause the *Booksmart* movie.

'So what's your status with Axel *now*?' Milly says, not even looking up from her screen.

'Why?'

'No reason. Just wondering if you're back together or not.'

'What did Axel say to you yesterday at the front door?'

I catch the side of her mouth quirk. Like she knows something. But it's a weird expression. And I don't know why, but when her eyes flash up at me, I quickly look back down to my phone and pretend to be engrossed with it. But I can't help myself. 'Yeah, thanks for telling him I was at Ella's house!'

She chokes. 'Uh, were you having an orgy there or something? Why shouldn't I tell Axel you were at your mate's house?'

I shake my head and don't answer. Because she's right. Axel shouldn't overreact to everything. He should trust me. I remember the lube sachets Axel – and Mum – found. '*You* seeing anyone right now . . . ?' I say, acting uninterested – like it doesn't matter to me either way.

Milly doesn't reply. So I kick her.

'Ow!' She kicks me back.

'I said, are you seeing anyone right now?'

'Yeah, I know you did,' she says. 'Axel dumps you and suddenly you want my life story.'

Eh? 'He didn't— I'm just asking what you're up to!'

'Are you . . . ?'

'Yes! You're my sister. We talk about stuff.'

'What stuff?' she jibes.

Uh?

'Exactly. You're a narcissist. Own it. Don't suddenly pretend you're interested in other people at this stage in your career. It doesn't suit you.'

This stuns me.

But then I hear the front door and Mum bustles through with the takeaway food, saying, 'Help get the plates and chopsticks and things, will you?'

Aghast at being called a narcissist, I don't get off the

sofa. Milly swings her legs past me and goes to clatter plates and glasses out of the cupboards. Am I a narcissist? What makes someone a narcissist? Since when does Milly even know what that means? I don't even know what it really means. Vain? That I'm vain? Caught up in myself – in what I want? Is that *really* so bad?

I made Axel go to RCA yesterday. He did that for me. Even though I lied about going to Ella's. Is that why he was seething all the way through the film? Because, yet again, I'm so caught up in *myself* – so rigid – that I don't give him the chance to be *himself*?

Milly just nudges back in between me and Mum on the sofa without a care, and sits there slurping, eating with her mouth open and licking her fingers.

When Dad comes home by the end of the film, I give him my barely touched plate to heat up in the microwave and tell them I'm not feeling well. I go to my room, curl up in bed and search *how do you know if you're a narcissist?*

I take a test. The result: *'You Have Minimal Narcissistic Tendencies'*.

Even though this gives me some relief, I still doubt it and retake the test repeatedly until I finally get the score up, just tipping me into the Mild Narcissistic Tendencies category. This makes me feel a little better. Perhaps because I'm being honest . . .

CHAPTER 16

LISS

I miss the bus. The moment I've fantasised about all night. The person. Seeing her. Again. Being with her for those few minutes alone on *our* bus, before George joins us at the next stop. And what do I do? Sleep in, spend too long second-guessing how she prefers my hair, and miss the bus and her!

I should've messaged her last night. I should've just done it. I know it wasn't by accident that she held my hand. I know it wasn't just a friendship thing . . .

Please don't let it be a friendship thing! Please be into me. What sort of girl is she into? Mhairi McIntyre. Mhairi was her type. Clever. In top sets alongside her. Able to talk about feminism and women's rights. Out. Big boobs. A brunette . . .

I glare at the end of my blonde fishtail plait and blank

my B cups, to open my messages again in case she's DM'd me. Nothing.

I could message her . . . Send a face-palm that I missed the bus. I could ask her to sign me in, so I don't get a warning for being late. Why would she do that though? We're not even in the same classes.

If only I'd said something in the jacuzzi. What sort of loser just sits holding someone's hand and says nothing? Nothing! Maybe she thinks she was wrong. She probably thinks she was wrong! Wait – I'm the one who's wrong. Why would she be into me? I'm that dumb blonde who didn't even realise she liked girls until last year. Who never speaks up, never knows what to say. Isn't well read. Struggles to read! Needs extra time in her exams. Sporty. Yes. We have that in common. A match. Equal on the pitch. But that's all I've got. Is that enough?

As for my ex: Ijeoma doesn't even like Axel! That face she pulled when Eve was worrying over Tavi the other night. Saying she thought there was something more to why Tavi and Axel had broken up . . . Ijeoma had replied, *'I'll forgive those straight girls two dates with Mr Vain. The first, they're blinded by his pretty face so they'll inevitably go in for a second. But surely by the end of that second date they've clicked he's a misogynist. Even the intellectually challenged ones should be running for cover after the third!'*

Axel and I dated immediately before Tavi. Who else could Ijeoma have been referring to? And even if she meant random straight girls, she clearly thinks I'm stupid.

ELLA

'We could work on the misogynistic make-up material again tonight?' I say to Mum as she pulls up at the school entrance. 'I'm supposed to be going to this lame book-club thing, but I can ditch it . . . ?'

'You're in a book club?' Mum says incredulous.

'Eh, yeah. That's not *that* surprising, is it?'

'No . . . Apart from the fact you made me find YouTube videos of actors reading your bedtime books when you were little because you said reading was boring. And you said I didn't *read it as good as Rik*.'

'That was your fault for putting a four-year-old in front of Rik Mayall reading Roald Dahl!'

'Classic!' Mum says simply.

'So do you want to work on the make-up routine? I was researching last night and some of the background to these names. It's crazy who chooses them! And it all started in the nineteen eighties. I've brainstormed a few ideas already. But I thought we could maybe use them like prompts. I've got a list. And we can vibe off each other. To take it further?'

'Not tonight. I need some time to think it through myself. Go to your *book club*.'

'Okay . . . But you'll run it by me, you know, before it's finished?'

'Eh, okay?'

I say, 'It's just, there's lots of other brands. They're not all totally sexist.'

Mum says, 'Obviously.'

'You should see the influencer-endorsed eyeshadow and highlighting palettes. They're another breed of inspirational, *be the best you can be* shit.'

Mum smiles but it doesn't reach the side of her mouth for long.

'I thought you were going to let me help you on this,' I say, rapidly realising that things are slipping back to our usual detachment-parenting routine.

'You've already helped. I just need to work out whether this really fits into my image right now,' Mum says.

'Right.'

'Don't be like that, Ells Bells.'

I open the car door. 'I'll get an Uber back tonight. Just in case you're out,' I say, and slam the car door behind me. I should've known she wouldn't want me to work alongside her. She always wants the attention for herself. It's always about her.

TAVI

I perch on the edge of the canteen bench opposite Ella at lunch, rest my tray on the table and rush, 'We can't have Bu–ook Club at mine tonight. We need to postpone. Axel's coming over.' I keep an eye on the door for him, ready to engage my thigh muscles and shift to *our* table. Axel can't see me with Ella and Larissa and all the other Buzz Club members.

Ella double-takes and scowls at me. 'We're not cancelling tonight's meeting! Eve's just recruited four new members and anyway, everyone's brought their vibes into school! You did, didn't you?'

'I've got mine,' George says. 'I even put in new batteries.'

Larissa, Eve and Ijeoma affirm they have theirs too.

'See, Tavi, George put new batteries in hers especially,' Ella says sarcastically. 'Anyway,' she continues, 'it's time we got things moving to the next level . . .'

I don't hear what the next level entails because Axel pushes in through the canteen's swing doors and I practically levitate and relocate to our usual lunch table, desperately racking my brain for an excuse to tell him.

'Sorry, I can't. Mum's cooking a family tea.'

'Lucky David's always telling me I'm like a son to him then,' Axel says.

I fidget, shifting the dog tag pendant. 'Not tonight, Axel,' I say firmly. Keeping focused on the dining table, to avoid seeing his anger. Waiting it out in silence.

'Fine,' I hear in this monotone, cold voice. 'I'll stay home all alone.'

I shrug my shoulders up and slap on a smile, looking hyper bright around the canteen. This is what Milly meant. Me being selfish. If I really cared for Axel I'd go out and meet him tonight. Or I'd cancel Buzz Club so he could come over instead.

I am a narcissist.

ELLA

'I can't tonight,' I say to Maz, as he stalks me on my way to Modern Studies, last period. 'I've joined this lame-ass book club that Tavi's set up. Got to fulfil sole-friend duty and turn up.'

'Do you *have to*? Axel wants me to go with him and Neil to Dawson Park. But I'd rather spend time with you.'

'Go. I'm not free.'

'You're never free,' Maz mopes. 'I'm starting to think there's something wrong with me . . .'

What's with all the needy? But because his pout's so cute, I throw the boy a bone. 'I can come over after Book

Club. I'll edit your Bloat Burger video. Leave your window open.'

'Yeah? That would be great.' He lights up like his PlayStation.

'Mhm. In fact, I might show you my new purchase, if you're lucky.'

'Oh yeah?' He tugs on the back of my school bag to make me stop. 'What've you been buying?' he asks.

I suck my teeth and then grin at him. 'It's a surprise!'

'I *love* surprises.'

'I know you do.' I let Maz lean down and kiss me slowly like I'm sweet. He's in one of his romantic moods. Maybe I will leave Buzz Club early. Least this boy knows how to make a girl feel wanted.

'Maz!' I hear from along the corridor. I pull back and see that it's Axel and he's with some younger girls.

Maz doesn't look at him though. He's fiddling with a button on my school shirt, and murmurs, 'You promise you'll come over . . . ?'

'I said I would.'

'You said you *might*.'

'Maz! You're coming to Dawson Park tonight, yeah?' Axel shouts.

'Promise,' I say, and stretch up to kiss him.

CHAPTER 17

TAVI

'Want me to order us some real food?' Ella says, curling her lip at the plate of crudité veggies and houmous Mum's made for a Book Club snack.

I ignore Ella and offer the next of my fifteen 'guests' something to eat. 'There's pizza slices and sausages coming,' I add.

'Aw, yum!' George says.

'Thanks, Tavi!' Eve says.

Just call me the hostess with the mostess. Mostest vibrators in her room, more like. Everyone's just sitting waiting with a vibrator in one hand and a carrot or cucumber stick in the other.

I scan my anti-mother-barricade against my bedroom door and thank the universe Mum agreed to send Milly to Anusha's house straight after school.

My mood: I'm flipping between seething that Ella's put me in this vibrator-in-the-house situation yet again (fifteenfold more) and secretly happy I gave in to hosting so I can spend more time with this group of girls. Selfish or not, I like the way they're making things feel lighter and brighter in here.

Ella flips my mood to pissed off again when she acts like she owns the place and pushes between bodies to dump down her Louis Vuitton weekender bag in the middle. She even sits on my swivel desk chair to flick through her femual. What a stupid fucking name for a pink, glittery notebook!

'Right,' Ella says. 'We'll start with some housekeeping. Namely, this is officially *Book Club*. So we need some books!' She leans forward and unzips her bag to reveal it's full of books. How did she lug all those here? 'We can multitask,' she explains. 'These are homework as well as your cover story. Take your pick.'

George pulls out *The Art of War*. She pouts and raises her eyebrows and then shrugs. 'Have you got an audio book for it?'

Ijeoma lucky-dips the bag and lifts out *Sex and the Single Girl*. She holds it up. 'Any takers?'

'Let me look at the back . . .' Eve says.

Ijeoma dips in again. Looks at the title – *The Second Sex* – and passes that book onwards. The next, she passes to me: *Come as You Are* by Emily Nagoski.

'Err, thanks,' I say to Ijeoma, and then awkwardly turn my smile to Ella. She's the one who's buying us gifts all over again. And this time it feels like they're totally befitting a secret feminist club.

'There's one in there especially for you, Ijeoma,' Ella says, swinging my chair from side to side.

'Oh yeah?' Ijeoma says warily.

'Yeah.' Ella dips into the bag. 'Here.' She holds it out: *The Lesbian Body* by Monique Wittig. Ijeoma doesn't take it. I side-eye between Ella and Ijeoma. I don't know if this is an insult or a legit, considerate gift. With Ella, even good intentions tend to be as subtle – and as welcome – as a brick to the forehead. 'It's hard to get hold of,' Ella adds. 'You might already know its French title – *Le Corps Lesbien*. Don't worry, it's not about sapphic necrophilia!' She creases up at her lame joke.

'Ella . . .' Larissa sighs.

'What? Don't tell me you want to read it too!'

'No!' Larissa protests.

'Great. Thanks, Ella,' Ijeoma says smoothly. 'You can borrow it after me.'

'I thought you made me chairperson?' I say.

'Yeah?' Ella snips. 'Act like one then.'

I snap back, 'Get out of my chair then!'

'Aggy!' Ella says, vacating the chair and grabbing up her Louis Vuitton from the floor.

I take possession of my throne.

Ella's muttering as she searches through her bag, 'I go to all the trouble of planning out a totally revolutionary reading list for Book Club and . . .' She removes two books and chucks them in my lap and then tips the remaining books into the middle of the circle, dumps her bag on my desk and pushes in by Larissa on my bed.

I look at the top book in my lap: *Vagina*. And turn over the other to look at its cover – *Disarming the Narcissist* by Wendy T. Behary, LCSW . . .

It takes a few seconds to cross my synapses. 'What the actual fuck, Ella?'

'What?' Ella gets up and peers at my lap. 'Oh . . .' she says easily. 'How did *that* get in there?' She looks around everyone else, as if one of them slipped it in the bag. Then shrugs and says to me, 'Might be worth a read?'

ELLA

I take the Vagina and Narcissist books from Tavi – ungrateful much – chuck them on her desk and clap my hands. 'Let's get to business. Everyone got their vibes out? New girls, tell us about yours next meeting. Tavi, where's your vibrator? Come on!'

Why did I make her chairperson? It should be me. This

lot might not like me now, but they'll come round once they hear what I've got planned for us. Once they understand how big this club is going to be. This is my show! My revolution! Just you wait and see what I'm capable of, girls. Mother! 'Two things you love about your vibe. Come on, Tavi!'

Everyone turns to Tavi expectantly.

Tavi glares at me. Sulking over the books? That was a legit attempt to help the girl out of a toxic relationship. Or has she *still* not used her vibrator?

But she surprises me and steps between legs to lift the bottom drawer out of her bedside table, to retrieve the neoprene case of that elite vibrator. I should've kept that one for myself. She doesn't even realise what I gave her. It's like giving someone an Aston Martin and they scrape the wheels on the pavement when they go through the McDonald's drive-through . . . Fucksake.

'That's such a good idea,' Eve says to Tavi. 'Storing it under the drawer!'

'Depends if you plan on using it or not!' I snap. 'Mine lives under my mattress for easy access.'

'What about when your mum changes the sheets?' one of the new girls says.

I shrug. 'We have a cleaner for that.'

No one gets a chance to acknowledge me properly because she asks Liss next. 'Where do you keep yours?'

'Uh . . . In a packet of Bodyform – an empty one. Mum's freaked out by periods. So, she won't look . . .' Liss gives up on her stammering with a shrug. What's wrong with her?

'How can she be freaked out by periods?' George says. 'How can you be *female* but freak out over periods?'

Liss turns a deeper shade of red and shrugs.

'My mum's worse. She's like a sniffer dog!' Eve pipes up. 'She found the condoms I got from Sex Ed – you know, the class they do in Year Nine – literally the very next day, while I was at school. I'd hidden them inside this Japanese puzzle box my granddad gave me! And when I came home the condoms were just sitting on the top of my desk with a note that said, "We need to talk!" She didn't believe me about the class and ended up calling school to check. Then she blamed me for hiding the note from school telling her the talk was happening. She finally found the school's notification email sitting in her junk folder.'

Eve's not so bad. A bit keen maybe. But it's good she's well into Buzz Club. Maybe I should make her the chairperson? She's popular. She's already introduced new members. I'll need help, if I'm going to take this club to where I want it to go.

'Guess we can cross off the discussion on where-to-keep-your-vibe from our proposed schedule,' I say. 'Shall we get back to tonight's agenda? Tavi?'

Finally, Tavi admits it. 'I haven't used mine yet.'

The newbies are surprised. The others groan. Getting them to agree to changing the chairperson's going to be a piece of piss.

'I'll start then,' I say. 'First thing I love about mine is that it's ombré! It adds this disco chic vibe . . . to my vibe.' I laugh. Yeah, this is meant to be fun, ladies. 'Which is really appealing and doesn't look cold and clinical like Tavi's medical-grade-silicone vibrator!'

TAVI

Medical grade? Distractedly, I unzip the case to look at my pebble-shaped vibrator. I suppose it does look clean and clinical. I can see why Anusha thought it was for hair removal on my birthday. I turn it the correct way round so the rounded tip falls into the sculpted recess of the case. And tuck the still-wrapped cable behind the elastic. Slide the instructions inside the pocket. I'm going to read those later. And put a little plastic square in the same place. There's another. I pick it up and glance at the others distractedly, they're laughing at something George said. And then I focus back on the square and read the hot-pink letters: *GLIDE*.

Shit!

It wasn't Milly's lube that Douglas, Mum and Axel found. It's mine.

LISS

Ijeoma's next. I'm still cringing at admitting in front of her that I use a Bodyform packet to hide my vibrator. I can't even look at her face. All I can do is stare at her shoulder.

'It's called a Mini Magic Wand,' Ijeoma explains. 'I like the USB charger, because I can plug it into my laptop.'

'Why's that good?' George says confused. 'Because it's convenient to watch porn?'

I can't listen. Thinking about . . . Ijeoma using it. Wondering whether she— I can't. Not here, with them around.

Ella snorts. 'Ijeoma doesn't look at porn!'

'How do you know I don't watch porn?' Ijeoma says.

My eyes flick now to Ijeoma's face. My heart's thundering.

Ella stumbles, 'I suppose . . . Yeah, I mean there's loads of girl-on-girl.'

'There's loads of lesbian porn, Ella!' I blurt, so everyone looks at me sharply. I suddenly feel like I'm in a tunnel and I'm going to faint. 'It's different . . .' I add, redundantly trailing off and trying to look anywhere but at Ijeoma. My eyes track crossed legs, school skirts and end up randomly meeting Eve's eyes.

Eve puts her hands up in her defence. 'Don't look at me! I'm the one with Psycho Sleuth Mother, remember. I've only watched porn on Olly's laptop and he's not exactly into lesbian stuff.'

'Not that it's any of your business, Ella,' Ijeoma says, 'but I do watch porn. *Girl-on-girl*, as you put it. And yes, Liss, I also watch lesbian porn when I can find it.'

I'm dead. I'm officially expired.

'It's you straight girls I feel sorry for!' Ijeoma continues. 'Hetero porn's mostly filmed from the male's viewpoint. Personally, I don't see how any of you are turned on by looking at one but there must be *some* girls who want to look at a penis instead of a hairless vulva!'

Totally and utterly deceased. She's amazing. Spectacular! She's never, ever going to want someone like me.

'Tavi, you're our resident porn expert!' Eve says. 'You must've had to watch some seriously sick shit!'

'What?' Tavi says shocked.

Oh, Eve . . .

'You know – Axel. He's, like . . . addicted to porn. He's . . .' Eve trails off.

Tavi looks mortified.

Then George snorts. 'Ugh! Remember that video he sent round with the—' She must notice we've all fallen silent.

'Sorry, Tavi,' Eve blunders. 'I didn't mean . . . What you and Axel do in private, that's your—'

'Oh, Tavi doesn't *do* anything in private with Axel!' Ella says.

'Ella!' I warn.

'What?' Ella smirks. 'I'm only saying—'

'That's it!' Tavi lurches off her chair, livid. Like she's ready to slap Ella.

Ella gives her *innocent* wide eyes, daring her. I'm tempted to slap Ella myself.

But Tavi just shouts, 'Pizza!' Throws her vibrator case at her chair. Steps between the other girls to the door and kicks the jammed hockey stick and laundry bin out from below the handle.

'Take a joke, Tavi,' Ella drawls. 'Where are you going?'

'Oh, I'm getting *real food*, Ella. Weren't you listening? Don't want my *guests* to get hungry.' She gestures to the barely touched platter of raw veg and spicy houmous her mum sent up. 'Won't be long,' Tavi says, tight and bright. 'Ijeoma, carry on. You can fill me in on the other benefits of your . . .' she raises her voice as she opens the bedroom door, '*BOOK* when I get back!' and she pulls the door closed behind her.

CHAPTER 18

ELLA

'My turn,' George says, when everyone's still laughing over Khair's story about her long-sighted mum accidentally cleaning her teeth with the baby's nappy-rash bum cream. Yeah, they all laugh at that drivel but they never laugh at my jokes! 'So,' George continues, 'my first favourite thing about my vibrator is also a negative. It's—'

'Let me guess,' I say. 'Batteries!'

She scowls at me. 'Yeah it is, actually. It's a positive as well as a negative.'

Maybe I'll put hair-removal cream beside Mum's electric toothbrush for a laugh.

'The positive of batteries means I don't have to plug it in to charge – so there's no chance Mum'll find my vibrator charging like Khair's. But that's also a negative because I looked this up online and this one is totally budget – which should be a positive for cash-strapped teens – but did I mention that batteries are extortionate and you still haven't bought me rechargeables . . . ?'

Least everyone else is rolling their eyes at her now. Maybe George's endless droning on about batteries will bring them round to my side.

The bedroom door opens and we scuffle to hide our vibes. But it's only Tavi, with a plate stacked with little squares of pizza and a bowl of sausage pieces with toothpicks. I watch the others grab their allotted morsel, and by the time they get to me there's a single piece of pizza left that's half crust. And two sausage fragments. At least she'll never compete with my hospitality skills.

'Ella,' Tavi says, 'you're in my seat again.'

'I was keeping it warm for you,' I say dismissively. 'Okay, okay! I said we'll get you rechargeable batteries, George. What else do you like about your vibrator?'

'You better. Anyway the second thing – the best bit – is when I turn this right up, you just have to screw the battery cap on as far as possible and . . . it goes really, really fast!'

Her vibrator – the cheapest piece of junk me and Liss chose because there was all of a fiver left of my gift vouchers – has become a demented, shivering, hot-pink willy. I can't take my eyes off it. Imagining it'll explode any second – and I don't just mean that in a dodgy double-entendre way – I mean the thing looks like it's about to blow – err, detonate.

'Having it full speed does run the batteries down quicker,' George says.

'Enough with the batteries!' I say, still staring at the willy.

'Excuse me, grumpy guts, I was just about to explain I put brand-new ones in this morning so you could all see how powerful it can go! Want to feel?'

We pass it around. It makes my hand numb. But also, there's a weird power about it that's not just the new batteries. It literally feels loaded. Like a weapon.

'This is clean, isn't it?' Eve checks.

'Course it's clean!' George says indignant. 'Is yours?'

'Pristine,' Eve replies, putting the tip of George's vibrating willy against her nose. We have a go at that – it tickles then turns my nose numb too.

Ijeoma isn't keen and deflects it back to me.

'Does it go any faster?' I try to turn it tighter.

'That's the fastest,' George says. 'Pass it back. Also, another thing I'm not that impressed with is the noise. It's really loud compared with all yours.'

I grip the rubber shaft in my left hand and twist the battery lid at the base. I grip it harder and twist it round and round like I'm trying to open a nail-varnish bottle that's seized shut. 'Oh shit!'

'What?'

'It's jammed.'

'No, it isn't!' George says, grabbing it from me. She tries. And gives up angrily by throwing it towards Ijeoma.

Ijeoma yelps and kicks it across the rug to Tavi. The willy lies there wobbling and buzzing on the floor.

TAVI

Everyone squeals and shrieks, clearing around me like the floor's lava.

Worried Mum's going to appear because of the noise, I swipe up the rampant willy, block out its horrible fleshy sensation against my palm and try to unscrew the end. But it's well and truly stuck. Tight.

'Ella!' I say, and toss it to her. I grab my phone, flick through the Sonos app and press play on house music, and move the speaker to point at the bedroom door.

Ella's whacking the rubber vibrator against my headboard, like it's a flexible sword. Everyone else is creasing themselves in hysterics. Tears are threatening to flood my own face but, unlike the others, not through humour. How does this sort of shit keep happening *at my house*? Oh yeah – Ella! I drag a cushion from below Ella's knees, throw it on the ground, yank the vibrator away from her, toss it onto the cushion and stamp on it, but I mis-aim and my foot bounces off the rubber like the thing's a short, podgy trampoline.

'GIRLS!' I hear yelled through the music. I freeze. And . . .

. . . that's definitely a *knock* on my bedroom door!

I swing round, kick the vibrator behind me, everyone scrabbles across the floor grabbing up their own appendages and just as my bedroom door opens before me, I remember that I didn't replace the hockey stick under the door handle.

'Mum!' I shout. Though she probably can't hear me because the music is blasting.

'Turn the music down a bit!'

'Sorry!' I turn to the others. They're all sitting and lounging holding up Ella's Book Club reads or their phones. Larissa seems to be laughing behind a book called *The Beauty Myth* because, although she's covered her face, I can see her shoulders shaking like she's got hypothermia. 'I'm going to turn the music down,' I shout. 'Just a bit!' Please God, please God! Where have they put George's vibrator? That thing is really, really noisy, and if it's still buzzing . . .

I turn the speaker down a couple of notches.

'Quieter, Tavi!' Mum says.

'Okay . . . only, we were just about to make up another dance, weren't we! Burn off those snacks.' I point to the empty pizza and sausage dishes.

Mum looks at the bowls. At least, I hope that's what she's focusing on. I can't see any incriminating vibrating objects peeping out . . . apart from my neoprene case that's lying on the floor against my chest of drawers! For the love of giving-me-a-break please no more loose *GLIDE* lube packets!

'Yeah!' George jumps up and starts doing a really energetic version of YMCA, only it looks like she's just spelling out YMYM. She looks like a seagull.

'Thank you so much for the lovely, healthy snacks, Mrs Thompson!' Eve says, pointing to the lonely, still-full bowl of crudités on my chest of drawers. *Don't look at the chest of drawers, Mum!*

I move to turn the music down one more notch and then Larissa catches my eye. She's staring over her book cover at me so intently that I think her eyes might pop out of their sockets. I leave the music where it is.

'You have to turn it down soon, Tavi! Mrs Stanton'll call Noise Control like she did that time we were in the garden!'

'Okay!' I say.

'Thanks, Mrs Thompson!' George says, progressing on to some sort of Air Hostess Nearest Exit Signalling moves.

'Lovely to see you, girls! Maybe next time you can show me your dance routines downstairs. I was really good at the "WAP", wasn't I, Tavi?'

'Eh, yeah, you were . . .' I say weakly.

Everyone winces. Apart from Ella, who says, 'Go on, Mrs T, show us your "WAP"!'

'Next time!' I shout pointedly, nodding for Mum to leave.

'Fine. I'm going!' Mum retreats.

I follow her to the door, point a warning finger for the others to stay still, and go out onto the landing. I wave as Mum heads downstairs. When she disappears from view, I pad back and shut the door. 'Coast's clear!'

'Thank fuck for that!' George blurts.

'Can I turn this down now?' Eve yells.

'Yeah, turn it off completely!'

The music stops abruptly. And everyone looks at Liss.

She pulls the still furiously pulsating vibe out from below her school skirt, chucks it across the floor and puts her face in her hands with a whimper.

George and Ijeoma say together, 'Are you okay?'

'No!' Liss wails.

'Stop being dramatic,' Ella says.

'If you think I'm being dramatic, Ella!' Liss squawks. 'Let's see you sit on that *thing* for longer than a few seconds—!'

We can't get George's vibrator to stop.

Larissa's traumatised and says she never wants to see it again.

George is delighted because she says we now have to buy her a totally new one because hygiene is the second rule of Buzz Club and not only have we breathed on it, handled it and stamped all over it, but Larissa's sat on it, and if George takes it home her dad will hear it buzzing in her school bag.

Ella leaves first, saying she's off to see Maz. The others clear out rapidly after that. Not wanting to be left with the smoking gun in their hands. Larissa's the last person to get picked up by her mum and because she seems genuinely shaken, I tell her not to worry. I'll deal with it.

When she's gone, I pace round my room trying to work out the best method of disposal. I think about drowning it in the bath, but someone said theirs was waterproof so George's might be too. And what happens if you put batteries in water? Is it like electricity? Will I get a shock? Imagine I get a shock that kills me. And Mum, Dad and Milly find me face down in the bath with a hot-pink vibrator floating, buzzing, beside me! That's like those sex-games-gone-wrong stories you hear about. Who wants to be remembered as that girl who died in the bath with the vibrator? Because that sort of gossip's bound to get out! Hell, the way Milly's acting towards me right now – she'd make sure of it!

It has to be something else . . . ?

I could put it in the garden shed and hope those new

batteries run out quicker than expected – surely George bought cheapy batteries! But what if Dad needs something from the shed?

Then I think of it. The best idea.

I wrap the jumping and jerking vibrator in the most unobtrusive bubblewrap-lined brown envelope I can find in Milly's craft drawer. Tear Mum's name and address from the label on the front, just to be sure there's no comeback. Then I chuck it out the bathroom window into our side alley. I grab my house keys, shout to Mum that Liss forgot her book and I'm just meeting her on the corner, get outside, swipe up the angry package, and run all the way to the end of our street and halfway along the next, and shove it deep into a public bin. I can hear it buzzing furiously as I jog back, until it recedes to just a residual ringing in my ears.

CHAPTER 19

LISS

New Chat.

Ijeoma: Hey. You okay?

Me: Oh, hi! I think so. Earlier was . . .

Ijeoma: Traumatic?

I want to write '*very*'. Instead, I write:

Me: Unexpected?

> **Ijeoma:** That's one way of describing it.

> **Me:** Embarrassing? Perhaps that's more accurate.

> **Ijeoma:** For sure! I can't believe Ella got me talking about watching porn!

I didn't think Ijeoma got embarrassed. Ever. She's so confident. So in control. My stomach squirms remembering my own embarrassment at blurting *lesbian porn*.

> **Me:** I thought that was really honest and authentic – and brave! Not like me going all to pieces just because I sat on a vibrator.

> **Ijeoma:** Don't let Ella belittle your experience. I've noticed she does that to you a lot. I mean, you literally took one for the team back there!

Another message pops up before I can reply.

> **Ijeoma:** Sorry, I didn't mean to make light of what just happened.

> **Me:** It's okay. It's kind of funny when you put it like that. You know me – always a team player!

I send her a crazy-face emoji. She replies with a skull emoji.

> **Me:** Thanks for checking in on me.

Ella certainly hasn't bothered. She just left to see Maz without even a backward glance. I bite my thumbnail, contemplating whether tonight really was the last straw.

I start typing:

> **Me:** And you're right. That's Ella's and my thing. If she wasn't my oldest friend, I'd . . .

I press send before I can finish.

Ijeoma doesn't reply straight away.

I sit up against my pillows and stare at my phone. Hoping to see another *Ijeoma is typing* signal. I don't want this to be over. But I don't know what else to type to keep her here.

Then:

> **Ijeoma:** You don't fancy a run, do you?

A run . . . ? When?

> **Me:** Do you mean now?

> **Ijeoma:** Yeah. I could come past your house? Dawson Park's closed now but we could keep to the pavement streetlights or go down along the water?

I check the time – it's almost nine p.m. Far too late for a run. Too dark. And I've just eaten. There are many reasons to say no. I type:

> **Me:** Sure!

Adding:

Me: Who else is coming?

Ijeoma: Just me.

My stomach tips over the precipice, plummets and climbs again to dizzy heights. She can't know. Is this . . . ?

Me: Wait, you don't know where my house is!

Ijeoma: Tower Court.

How does she . . . ?

Me: The number?

Ijeoma: No. What number is it?

I pause. I don't know what I was thinking there. Of course she doesn't know the number of my house. She's not a stalker. Like me. The person who stares at her house on Google Maps every other day. She probably just saw me walk up my street post-hockey-match drop-off. Why am I even disappointed she doesn't know exactly where I live?

> **Ijeoma:** So? Do you fancy a run?

> **Me:** Sorry. Yes. Definitely!

> **Ijeoma:** Be with you in five. On the corner with Ralston Rd.

I hover. Racking my brain for a response that's relaxed but positive. And fail. So write:

> **Me:** Great. Be there in five.

Five minutes! I haul open my wardrobe doors and stare, paralysed with nerves, at my leggings and running tops. She once said she liked the burgundy Puma set. The top falls off my shoulder – is that a good thing? Will it make her want to touch my shoulder?

'I'm just going for a quick run,' I say at the bottom of the stairs, dressed in the burgundy. Mum and Dad are on a sofa each with their laptops on their knees. Empty plates from supper still on the rug.

'Okay,' Dad says distractedly.

'Won't be long.' I reach for the front-door handle.

Mum looks up and says, 'You're not going out now – you're barely back. And you just ate!' She checks her MacBook. 'It's after nine, Larissa!'

'I'll keep to the streetlights.'

'You're not even wearing a trail jacket. There was frost earlier!'

'Who are you meeting?' Dad says suspiciously.

'No one. Just a girl from running club . . . We'll keep to the main streets. Or go along Dundee Road – no one will come near us with all the cars going by.'

Mum looks to Dad for support.

'We're just going for a run before bed!' I say, trying not to sound as desperate as I feel. 'To help us sleep,' I add.

'Twenty minutes max,' Mum says with a sigh. 'Get your hi-vis jacket and head torch!'

I don't debate. I grab the acid-yellow jacket and torch from the hall cupboard and escape outside.

I run down the hill and round the sweeping corner. And she's there. Stretching her hamstrings. She looks up. Waves. Bounces on her toes.

'Hey,' I say.

'Hi,' she says. 'Want to run anywhere specific?'

'Somewhere with plenty of lights?' I suggest.

'Course.' She smiles. The little gap between her front teeth is more prominent in the encroaching darkness. 'You putting that on?' she asks.

'Mhm?'

'Hi-vis,' she says, tugging at her grey reflective jacket by way of clarification.

'Oh, yeah.' I pull on my luminous jacket, hesitating before I zip it shut. So much for the Puma showing off my shoulders. And burgundy and acid-yellow! I probably remind her of a fire engine.

'Head torch is a good idea,' she says. 'Better than this thing.' She clicks on the light on her reflective body strap.

'My gran gave me it for Christmas . . .'

'Yeah?'

'Mhm,' I say. Is this what they mean by a lingering look? She's just staring at me. Is she going to kiss me . . . ?

'Are you wearing it?' she finally asks. 'The torch.'

I look at the elastic headband in my hand. 'Uh. Yeah, I . . .' I fix it onto my forehead. Imagine if I'd leant in to kiss her there, and she'd recoiled. Horrifically mortifying. What am I thinking? This is just a run! I turn my light on and Ijeoma's jacket glows, reflecting the beam like she's a character in *Tron*.

'Need to warm up?' she says.

My eyes flick across her silvery arm, imagining it wrapped around me – keeping me warm. I look down the hill to hide my blush and shrug. 'Unless you're already warm?'

'We could stretch at the sea-eagle sculpture?' she suggests. 'Then run on past the sailing club, over the footbridge and circle back round?'

The cycle path to the sea-eagle sculpture runs along the side of the water. There are no streetlights. It's totally dark at this time of year and night.

She reads my hesitation as she sets her smartwatch. 'Or we could just go along . . . ?'

'Sure,' I hear myself say. 'Sea eagle onwards sounds good!'

We set off slowly at our normal running-club warm-up pace. Usually it feels frustratingly slow, like we're speed walkers, but tonight I wish I could dial it back further. I want to remember every microsecond with her. Replay them later, alone.

Down on the main road we wait for a white van to pass, jog across when it's clear and turn along the road bridging the rail track. She slows so we take the pedestrian steps down to the beach together. 'Okay?' she says.

'Yeah,' I answer, briefly checking over my shoulder at the bottom, to scan the shadows for anyone lurking, and set off after her.

My torch is the best light down here. There's a glow from the streetlights up on the road but it's not reaching the shadows created by the bushes . . . or that bin. I'm acutely aware of our surroundings. Conflicted that it's good to be here, alone, with Ijeoma. This is what I've fantasised about for weeks, months, secretly. But also alert. Aware anyone could be down hiding on the beach, round that corner. We're vulnerable. Two girls. It never crossed my mind to check the darkness when I was with Axel. Or if I did, we laughed about it. And he said he'd protect me.

Why am I thinking of Axel? I'm here with Ijeoma! This is different. That's all.

We stride on, our pace increasing as my legs, now warmed, try to forget Axel. She matches me. We're equals. That's how it should be. Even the soles of our trainers drum a squeaky harmony on the tarmac.

And then we're here. At the sea-eagle sculpture. Safely. But all too soon.

I've stretched so much that my limbs are practically dangling from my joints, but still we haven't set off in the direction of the sailing club.

Ijeoma's torch-lit silhouette, on the far waterside of the sea-eagle wing, gives me away every time I look at her.

'Ready?' I say reluctantly.

'Not really . . .' she says.

I move towards her. 'You okay?'

The beam from my head torch makes her wince. She sinks lower, her back leaning against the long, elegant feather. 'Cramp. Can you flex my— Ah . . .'

'Oh! Here, sit.' I take her arm and help her hop to the nearest metal bench, and crouch before her to flex the sole of her trainer against the heel of my hand. 'Push against me.'

She pushes gingerly against me.

'Is it too sore?'

'Yes!' she gasps.

I wrench off her shoe and dig my thumb into the arch of her foot, only guessing at where she might be cramping. 'Is it there?'

'Hmhm!'

'Does that help?'

She winces in the beam of my torch again, but I realise it's not the light causing the discomfort. She nods quickly that it's helping. I work up the length of her foot with my thumb, grasping it tight, waiting until she tells me the pain has released her. This isn't a scenario I've imagined, while lying in the darkness below my duvet at night, with only her Instagram and TikTok accounts illuminating my fantasies. She has long toes like me. I hadn't realised I could be into feet. Because I must be. What this is doing to me . . . The thrill. The squirming, tension. But then, girls' feet are prettier than boys' . . .

Don't think about Axel's disgusting hooves!

I scrunch my eyes to refocus on the now. I'm down by the beach. In the darkness. Massaging Ijeoma's foot!

My thumb eases from deep dig to therapeutic massage, running from her heel, up her arch onto the ball, pausing there to knead it gently, not daring to blind her again with my torch, not daring to check her expression . . . What if she doesn't want me to do this? What if she thinks I'm a foot fetish creep and she's in too much pain to tell me to stop?

And in the very moment I realise I'm being completely inappropriate, we both recoil with fright as a high-pitched *TING* splits the air between us. Then another. *TING!* And another. *TING!*

'I think that's yours,' Ijeoma says.

I touch my breast pocket and struggle to get into the zip for my phone. I can feel it pulse with the continuing *TING*s. It's my Find My iPhone app. I cancel its alarm. And discover alongside it a missed call and two text messages from Mum.

> **Mum:** What are you doing down by the beach? You said you'd stick to the streetlights! Get home now!

> **Mum:** I'm sending your dad to come find you in 2 minutes, Larissa!

She messaged ten minutes ago! I look urgently back along the path, and hit call. Mum answers immediately. 'What are you doing down on the beach?' she shouts.

'Nothing. We're just stretching at the sea-eagle sculpture.'

'I told you to stick to the lights!'

I get to my feet. And say, 'I know. I'm sorry . . .'

'Are you really with a girlfriend, or is it a boy?'

'I'm . . .' I step away from Ijeoma towards the metal wing and duck behind it as if it's going to shield her from the lie I'm about to tell Mum. 'Just a girl from running club.' I can't use the word girlfriend in front of Ijeoma. 'We thought it was a good route down by the beach. She got cramp.'

'I don't believe you.'

'Mum.' This is mortifying. 'I'm with a girl from running club. We'll come back now. Dad hasn't left, has he?' Ijeoma's going to think I'm so childish. Her mum's probably never Find My iPhoned her in her life!

'What's her name?'

I hesitate before mumbling, 'Ijeoma.'

'Never heard of her.'

I cringe, not knowing how to respond. I can't let Ijeoma

know I've never spoken about her in front of my parents. That the reason I haven't is because I wanted to keep her name a precious secret. She'll get the wrong impression. Think that I'm not interested. I need her to know I'm interested. So interested!

Thankfully, Mum just goes off. 'You're lucky your dad had already gone for a shower otherwise I'd really have sent him to find you by now!'

'We're coming back,' I say, adding, 'but Ijeoma's got cramp so we'll have to walk.' And I hang up. Walk round the metal screen, cramming my phone in my pocket. 'Sorry,' I say. 'I have to head home.'

Ijeoma gives me a closed-lip, wincing smile under the beam of my head torch.

Yeah, I bet you wish you hadn't asked me to go for a run now. You'll never ask me again, will you. 'Has your cramp eased?' I ask.

'It has,' she replies simply.

'Okay. Shall we head back?'

'I could probably jog a little. I don't want your parents to be mad at you.'

'You sure?'

'Yep. Come on.'

We jog, slower than our warm-up, past the sailing club, over the rail track footbridge, along the main road and up the road parallel to Fairfield Road, Ijeoma's road. All the while, I'm aware Mum's probably tracking me via my phone. Waiting and watching for me to stop off or deviate. Ruining what could have been the best night of my entire life. Tonight could've been the start of everything! Something! I'm close to tears as we jog towards the turn-off for her road with the heart-shaped iron railings round the perimeter of her garden.

But then she doesn't stop. Instead, we continue jogging till the next junction and take the familiar turn down onto Ralston Road, slowing so that we're walking by the time we're down the hill, and on my little winding street.

'Do you want to come in and say hello?' I say, unsure why she's coming all the way home with me.

'Do you want me to?' she says as we pass from the bright streetlights into the dappled shadow of an overhanging tree.

'You don't need to. Mum's . . . fine.'

I see her nod out of the corner of my eye. And I realise I should've seen her home safely. She was the one who had cramp.

'Sorry I upset your parents,' she says. 'We'll go running at a better hour next time.'

'Next time?' I turn to see her grinning at me.

'Unless,' she shrugs, 'I'm just a girl from running club?'

I stare at her.

'You know what,' she says, stepping closer to me into

the shadows, 'I've been wanting to do this all night,' and she leans forward.

I hold my breath.

And then she takes my head torch off my head and turns it to shine directly in my eyes so that I'm blinded.

'Oh, sorry!' I say, stepping back with embarrassment, merging with a bush, losing my balance and falling into the bouncy branches.

She grabs my hand and we slowly pull against one another until I'm upright, and then suddenly it's dark.

She's turned my torch out. Or the battery has failed.

And we're still gripping one another's hands even though I've found my feet. And then, very slowly, I feel her shift our linked hands upright. And her fingers weave through mine. And suddenly, in the shadowy darkness, her lips meet mine.

CHAPTER 20

ELLA

I finish the lip liner on Maz's cupid's bow.

He pouts. 'Do I look pretty?'

'Haven't finished yet.' I look through the Nars lip glosses I stole from Mum's cupboard last week, hold up two for him to choose from. 'Shimmering beige-gold or peachy-pink? What's it gonna be?'

'Don't mind. You choose.'

'One'll hurt and the other will take you to heaven.'

Maz squints. 'Heaven, please.'

'*Orgasm* it is then.' I unscrew the wand and turn the base to him so he can see the label on the bottom of the tube. I slick the wet, sticky pink gloss along his bottom lip. Wish mine were as plump.

He manages to ventriloquist, 'Wha– wa e othe– hne call . . . ?'

'What's the other called? *First Time*.'

Maz frowns like he doesn't believe me.

'Look!' I show him the other label. 'The whole industry's fucked up. Nars make these. And on their website they call their customers *NARSissists*. Like it's funny. Like they've got a right to joke about being a narcissist because it sounds like Nars.'

Maz nods and then licks his lip. 'What's a narcissist again?'

'It's a legit personality disorder. It's like if you think you're the most important person in the world and you don't really care about anyone else.'

Maz pouts again and I lean forward and kiss him. 'You're so clever,' he says. 'I don't know any of these things.'

'You're the only one who thinks I'm clever,' I say, and lie back against his pillow. 'Everyone else thinks I'm gobby.'

'Everyone knows you're clever, Ells!' he says, lying down to face me. His big hands tucked under his cheek. 'Remember we used to try and copy your answers in Maths cause we knew you'd have your sums right?'

This makes me smile. Remembering how tight we all used to be – me, Liss, Maz and Axel – when we were younger.

'And the boys only call you gobby because they're scared of what you'll say next. To shut you up. You're always the one to call people out on their shit. It's a good thing.' Maz touches my hair.

I blush a little at hearing something nice about me. 'Yeah, it's a mess,' I say about my hair.

'It's not a mess,' he says thickly. 'It's soft.'

'Fluffy?'

'Silky curls,' he says, arranging it on the pillow with his fingertips. 'Like Sleeping Beauty's.'

'Unconscious? That's creepy, Maz.'

'Why don't you like me saying you're beautiful?'

'Okay. Tell me I'm beautiful then!' I pull a fugly face.

He smiles and leans forward but hovers above my contorted mouth.

Up so close, I can only just make out as he mirrors my *delightful* expression then kisses me with lopsided sticky-gloss lips.

Gotta love this boy. Even though I know I'll inevitably break him, in heart and spirit.

'So what's the book you're reading in Book Club?' he says, snuggling beside me. 'Read me some of it . . . ?'

I laugh again. At the thought of just telling him the truth. What do I owe the girls? None of them appreciate that Buzz Club was my idea. None of them appreciate me buying them vibrators. They'd rather have someone utterly clueless as their chairperson. Someone who wouldn't even know an orgasm if it smacked her in the flaps! They haven't any idea what we could achieve with Buzz Club if they just listened to me!

So I decide . . . fuck it.

I slide my hand below his pillow and retrieve my vibrator. And hold it up. 'This is the book.'

Maz frowns.

'*This* is the book. My book. Everyone else has one too. This is the *book*.'

He narrows his eyes. 'This is the book . . .' he repeats.

'It's a secret vibrator club, honey. There are *no* books. Well, actually, I did buy them books too but the club is all about vibrators.'

TAVI

I lie-in in the morning, lazily picturing my room filled again with all the personalities of Buzz Club. When I get to replaying Ella whacking George's vibrator against my headboard, I have to laugh. And shift to sit up against the wall. Last night was like a triple shot of life! Crammed, chaotic and fun . . .

I throw a glance towards my photos of Axel and me, and get up.

Downstairs, I find Dad sitting at the kitchen island with the remnants of his breakfast. He's usually left for the workshop by now. 'Morning, princess, how was your book club last night?'

'Eh, yeah, it was good . . . ' I say distractedly. 'Why are you still here?'

'Your mum wants us to have a chat.'

'A chat?' Immediately every possible thing I could be in trouble for flashes through my head. *Last night's Buzz Club. Ella's birthday gift. Those lube packets.* What else?

Mum appears through from the utility. 'I need you to watch Milly like a hawk today. Straight back here after school!'

'Err, why?'

'Milly—!' Mum yells, ignoring me. 'Get your backside down here now. I want a word with you!'

I look between my parents. 'What's she done?'

Dad shakes his head. 'We don't know yet.'

I hear Milly shout, 'I'm getting ready!'

Mum stalks to the door and bellows, 'Now—!'

'Okay . . . !' Milly comes down the stairs with half her hair straightened and the other half frizzy. 'What?'

'Where were you before curfew last night?'

'At Anusha's . . . ?'

'No, you weren't. Anusha's mum just messaged me. Anusha told *her* she was here!'

I side-eye Mills. Where was she last night?

'Where were you, Milly?' Mum repeats.

'Me and Anusha went to the swings in Dawson Park,'

she protests. 'Then we got chips. We weren't doing anything wrong. I got back here before nine.'

'You know your curfew's eight on a school night!' Mum says.

Milly fires back, 'You literally told me not to come home—!'

Dad glances at Mum to see if that's true – guilt washes over me that the only reason Mills stayed out was because I didn't want her knowing about Buzz Club – and then Dad says grimly, 'There was a bomb scare up the street last night.'

Startled, Mills and I say, 'A bomb—?'

'We need to know where you are, girls. All the time. Just in case there's an emergency. To keep you safe!'

'What kind of bomb?' Mills says.

'Where?' I say.

'Balbeggie Terrace. There was a police cordon – so your dad went to see what was going on. Tell them, David.'

'The polisman was being cagey, telling me to stay back – they'd evacuated all the residents. Poor souls had to schlep up the street in their dressing gowns and slippers to spend the night in the community centre. When I saw this bloke in a green spaceman suit and realised he was bomb squad. So the polis admitted what had happened.'

'What *had* happened?'

'Turned out a man was walking his dog before bed and heard buzzing coming from one of the bins . . .'

'Taviii—!' Eve calls to me, just as Mum and Dad pull away from dropping Milly and me outside school.

I glance at Milly. 'I'll see you later.'

Milly arches an eyebrow. 'I'm not going anywhere. Mum said you had to keep an eye on me . . .'

'Not in school.'

'We're not *in* school yet.'

'Stop being a weirdo. Hey, Eve. Oh, hey, Ijeoma, Liss, George . . .'

'Why the radio silence?' Eve says. 'Tell us what happened after we left!'

I glare at Milly. 'Go away.'

'I'm happy here,' Milly says. 'What happened after they left? Where did they leave from? Were you all at our house last night? Hey, Liss! How are you?'

'Hi, Milly!' Liss says, adding pointedly, 'This is Tavi's *little* sister, everyone!'

'Oh,' George says. Hopefully understanding not to say anything more about last night.

'Little . . . ?' Milly sneers.

'Okay, you've said hi to the big girls,' I say. 'Look, here's Anusha! Go play with your friend.'

The others smile, waiting for Milly to bog off.

'Uh . . . hi, Tavi!' Anusha says when she comes alongside us, for some reason avoiding eye contact with the others.

Ijeoma says, 'Morning . . . !'

'Um, yeah, hi!' Anusha waves quickly and grabs Milly's arm. 'We're late for— Bye then. Nice to . . . Bye!' And pulls Milly towards the school gates.

'Sorry, my sister's behaving like a weirdo at the moment,' I say in explanation.

'How old is she?' Ijeoma says. 'And her friend?'

Ella's voice booms from nowhere, 'Hello, Book Clubbers!' We all turn to see her with Maz. 'What're you doing?' she demands.

'Milly's fifteen,' I tell Ijeoma. 'Anusha's probably the same, I don't know, they're both Year Eleven . . .'

Ella raises her voice. 'We're not supposed to call Book Club meetings without notifying everyone, you know!'

'Oh, shut up, Ella!' Liss snaps. 'We're *literally* saying good morning! And since when have you ever done what you're supposed to?' Liss steps between us. And Ijeoma, George and Eve follow her towards school.

I gawp after Liss. Ella seems as surprised as I am, but quickly hides it with a scowl and tucks her arm back through Maz's and says, 'Come on, Maz. Let's get coffee. We've been up all night shagging – you should try it sometime, Tavi!' And tugs Maz with her.

I stare for a moment. Trying to put in order what just happened and how I've managed to find myself standing on my own. I didn't even get to tell the others that after they left last night, I somehow succeeded in calling in the bomb squad and evacuating four streets of neighbours in their jammies.

ELLA

Over Maz's shoulder, I watch Eve drag Tavi across the common room to the rest of Buzz Club lying on the beanbags. They're squawking like a coven. Way to draw attention to yourselves, *ladies*! So much for us agreeing to keep things secret. Khair gives Tavi half her beanbag and they all huddle round her. We'll see the steam rising from the cauldron any second now.

'Babe,' Maz says, touching my foot. He nods to my right and I side-eye to see Axel's watching them intently too.

I *knew* this would happen. Next thing I know they'll be posting squad goals photos on social media with #buzzclubbitches4eva.

I glance back to Maz and point the tip of my index fingernail between my front teeth reminding him he promised to say nothing to Axel, or any of the boys, about Buzz Club.

He shakes his head imperceptibly, winks and says, 'Did you have fun at your *book club* last night, babe?'

'Yeah, it was *stimulating* conversation,' I say grinning at him.

A collective scream raises from the Buzz Club group. And practically the entire common room rubberneck round to stare at them. They're recoiling and rolling, pissing themselves in hysterics. Tavi's just sitting in the middle with a smirk on her face, pretending to look coy and embarrassed. Even Ijeoma – who has never once cracked a smile at anything I've said – is laughing so much that she's gripping Liss's hand. Then George stands up, motions like she has a willy, and is beating herself off, then she suddenly screams BOOM and throws herself back onto her beanbag. They all scream again and *shhh* each other guiltily.

I look to Axel. He's beetroot. He gets up and walks out of the common room.

'What was that about earlier?' I say, dumping my bag beside Liss in English, the period before lunch.

She's leaning her fingertips on her temple, pretending to catch up on this week's reading chapter of '*Gatsby*.

'I know you can hear me!' I say, and drop into my chair, making sure to jolt the desk.

She removes her hand but only to turn the page.

'Be like that then . . .' I drum my fingers on the desk. 'What exactly am I supposed to have done wrong that you're ignoring me? Hmm? Or do you not need me as a friend anymore now you've got *Ijeoma* to hold your hand!'

Liss looks up startled.

'Quiet, please!' Ms Amjad our teacher shouts from the front.

'What . . . ?' I say to Liss.

'Qui-et!'

LISS

She knows. How does she know? She wasn't even with us. She was sitting with the boys. If Ella saw Ijeoma hold my hand, then everyone must've seen . . . I have to tell her. There's nothing to tell. Not yet. Well, there is. Ijeoma kissed me! If Ijeoma was a boy, I'd tell Ella . . . Would I? I'm not sure I would now. She's been vile lately. And Ijeoma's right, I shouldn't have to put up with Ella's snapping and talking over me. Especially when I'm the only girl at school who really cares about Ella. Except maybe Tavi . . . And everyone's enjoying Buzz Club but she's *even more* offended. I thought that was the whole point of us starting the club! Friendships and solidarity. Support. *Owning our own orgasms.*

Ella needs to start owning her behaviour. To me. To everyone.

I flick through my book to get to the right page. Why should I hide who I am? Ella's my oldest friend. It's time she supported me back as much as I support her. Even if I'm going to have to *force* her into it! Have to force myself into it more like . . . Dare I?

I lean my head closer to Ella, barely breathing, and say low, so that the rest of the class can't hear, 'I liked it when she held my hand . . .' Then I lean in even closer, so that I'm practically whispering in Ella's ear. 'But not as much as I liked it when she kissed me last night.'

'Larissa!'

'Uh? Yes, Ms Amjad?'

'Take up the reading, please. First para, third page into Chapter Seven. Just in case you and Miss Chatterbox Konstantinou are too busy gossiping about boys . . .'

Ella laughs as we walk out of class. 'Imagine if Ijeoma *had* kissed you.'

Ella's careless attitude feels like a slap in my face, a shock through my system. I can't stop and just keep walking.

'Wait up . . . Liss!'

I said I'd meet Ijeoma for lunch. I'll go to Ijeoma.

'Liss, wait.' Ella jogs to catch me. 'When do you think we should organise the next Book Club?'

'Everyone's coming to mine tonight,' I say monotone.

'Since when? I didn't authorise that!'

'No,' I say, finally stopping. 'We did. Tavi agreed.' I can't help adding, 'She's our *chairperson*, isn't she!'

Ella narrows her eyes at me. I don't wait to hear any more, pivot and head for the canteen. She doesn't seem so keen to chat after that. I know she's angry though. Because she gets her main course quickly and even though I relent and wait for her, she goes off alone to choose her drink. So when Ijeoma and Eve wave at me, I head over to them for respite.

When I look back for Ella, I see her sitting down with Maz.

TAVI

'Tavi, you finished your lunch?' I follow his voice across the canteen table and see Axel looming behind Eve.

'Eh, yeah, sure.' I push the rest of my food to the side and close my cutlery.

'Let's go then.'

'Bye, everyone,' I say, extracting myself from the bench. 'I'll see you later.'

'See you tonight, Tavi!' George grins. She mic-drops her hand. 'Boom!'

'Remember we're discussing fantasy fiction tonight,' Eve says. 'We need you there, Tavi.' She glances briefly to Axel who frowns immediately.

'You coming or not, Tavi?' Axel grunts.

'That *is* the question!' Eve says.

'What'd you say?'

'Nothing, Axel. See you later, Tavi.'

I follow Axel out of the canteen. Waiting for the inevitable explosion. But it doesn't hit. Instead, he drapes his arm over my shoulder and pulls me to his side. We walk slightly out of synch, so that my hip and shoulder bump him with each step. Then I realise he has my upper body clamped.

'So, good family meal last night?' Axel asks.

Shit. He knows. 'Eh, it didn't really happen.'

'No? What did you do instead?'

'Uh . . . Ella brought round all of Book Club . . .' I stammer.

'So I heard. Why are they coming over tonight then? You're not getting through a book a night! You're not that fast a reader. I doubt Georgina Marston can even read!'

I wince at his venom. I really like George. I say quietly, 'It's at Liss's house tonight.'

His hand tightens its grip on my shoulder. 'So that's it then? You're encouraging her to break us up? I told you she's been hitting on me.'

I don't say anything.

'You need to choose between me and this book club. Do you hear me?' he says angrily.

'That's sore, Axel!' I prise his fingertips from my upper arm and try to slide out from below his grip.

'I don't get why you're being like this. You wanted us back together. You were the one who was upset.'

'I know.'

'Then show me you'd rather be with me than them . . .' He trails his fingers below my school-shirt collar and hooks the dog tag's chain. 'Meet me tonight instead.'

'Mum and Dad really have said we have to stay in tonight. So I won't even go to Book Club . . .' The sensation of his touch, grazing my bare skin, makes me squirm and at the same time . . . it's a thrill. As if he's tickling me all over: earlobe, spine, around my thigh. . . .

I close my eyes. I'm turned on. His hands slide around my neck, enclosing my jaw, thumbs on my chin. He kisses me. Slowly. Then deeper. Harder. His tongue, teeth and lips hungry for me. Pressing me backwards. Crushing us together so we're like one. Partners. A proper couple. I ignore the drawing-pin tops from the noticeboard behind, digging into my scalp. He's right. I do want to be with him. We're meant to be together—

The chain round my neck tightens. Like a garrotte. Cutting into my throat.

'A–xel—!' I twist away desperately, snatching my release. And something slithers down my cleavage to rest between my boobs. 'What the—' Gripping my neck, I look at Axel.

His hand's hanging in the air with the silver chain dangling from it, then he says, 'Look what you did! You broke David and Caroline's Tiffany & Co. necklace!' And he chucks it at me.

The chain crumples against me and falls with the slightest *chink* onto the floor. I stare at it.

'Larissa—' Axel suddenly says.

I turn.

'Oh, hey. Hi, Tavi!'

I can't even muster a fake smile.

'Oh dear! Did you break your lovely necklace . . . ?' Her long hair tumbles loose as she bends to retrieve my chain.

Axel says, 'Yeah. She did.'

I hold out my hand numbly, so Liss can place the chain there.

As she smiles at me, expecting me to do or say something – be grateful maybe – I feel the dog tag slide lower, slip below my waistband, and the metal pendant clunks onto the polished concrete.

Axel swipes it up and winds his arm round my shoulder. 'Come on, clumsy. See you around, Larissa.'

LISS

I've been feeling guilty about being annoyed at Ella. Of course she'd think I was joking about Ijeoma and I kissing. Why would she ever think that was true – if I've never told her how I feel inside?

She shouldn't have laughed though, or said what she said: 'Imagine if Ijeoma *had* kissed you.' Yeah, I can, Ella. That's *exactly* what I *have* been imagining. For months!

This time I'm going to put her right. Make her mindful of other people. Of me. Of Ijeoma. Everyone. To start being kind! Well, kinder.

Ella finally emerges from the production booth in the school theatre at quarter past four.

'Hi!' I say. 'Did you get my message?'

'No?'

'Everyone's coming to mine for seven tonight. That way we've got time to eat and do homework beforehand.'

'And you're telling me why?'

'Because . . . I thought you'd want to know?'

'I'm not coming to Buzz Club.'

I instinctively look around to see if anyone heard her say Buzz Club, but the theatre is empty. 'Fine,' I say coolly.

Marginally less snippy, she adds, 'Maz is coming over.'

'Okay . . .'

'You'll need this.' She edges the strap of her Longchamp tote off her shoulder and passes me her pink glitter notebook.

'What do we write in it?'

'Follow the format of the earlier meetings. Attendance. Minutes. Agenda.'

'You sure you don't want to come?' I'm confused that she doesn't want to take part. This is her creation. Her revolution.

'No.'

'Okay . . .'

She waves her hands to shoo me.

I turn and walk for the door, not really in the mood for confrontation now.

Then she says, 'So what's going on with you and Ijeoma? Are you lesbian now?'

I stop with a jolt, hugging the glitter notebook. 'I'm just me . . .' I say unsteadily.

'I'm not bothered if you *are*!' she says. 'I'd just like to know what's going on with my best mate. So? Are you and Ijeoma a thing? Or are you just *friends?*'

She barely gives me a chance to breathe and turn to look at her before she adds, 'I won't say anything to Maz. Axel will do his shit when he finds out you're lesbian though. His ego can't handle the double whammy of not being able to get a stiffy over Tavi, then finding out you're turning on the wifeys better than he is. But I'll champion whatever *this is*,' she flicks her fingers at me, 'just tell me how you're identifying?'

I stare at her for a moment. '*This isn't* anything for you to champion, Ella. I'm spending time with Ijeoma. I like her. I don't need to put a label on my life. You don't need to shout about anything or go on any sort of crusade for us. We're just . . . two people.'

'So you're bi? Pan?'

'Bye, Ella.'

'Bi!'

I head down the corridor, spelling out, 'B. Y. E!'

After a brief pause, she shouts after me, 'Love you!'

As I'm already at the swing doors to the lobby, I don't bother replying.

CHAPTER 21

TAVI

'Tavi! How did you break it?'

'I don't know, it just broke,' I say shakily, rearranging the Tiffany & Co. chain with the dog tag on the kitchen counter so that it appears whole again.

Mum looks at the links. 'I'm sure they can fix it. They'll probably just add a new link.'

'Are you sure?'

'Oh, Tavi! Don't cry. It's okay . . .' Mum moves round the island and hugs me, which makes me dissolve into full-on sobs. 'Come on, you silly sausage.' She rubs my arms. 'It's a special piece of jewellery but it was an accident. We'll fix it.'

'I didn't mean to break it.'

'I know you didn't – you're always so careful with your things,' Mum says. 'Milly's the one who breaks everything.

Let's have a cup of tea and you can tell me all about these books you've been reading in your book club. It sounded like you were having a blast with your new friends last night.'

I nod miserably. I *was* having a blast. And this morning in the common room too. I felt . . . included. *Seen*. Then Axel put me back in my lonely box.

I tell Mum we're reading *The Great Gatsby* because I know Ella and Liss have that for English, and Ella made me watch the movie with her the other day. So at least I know the gist of what happens. I don't think telling Mum the cover story that I'm reading *Vagina* and *Disarming the Narcissist* – which, incidentally, I'm not because I'm tired of Ella's toxic mind games – is going to be any more palatable than me telling her the full truth that last night I shoved a malfunctioning vibrator in the bin on Balbeggie Terrace and that was the suspicious package the bomb squad *deactivated* in a controlled explosion and took away for analysis. And, just maybe, they'll find my, Milly's and Mum's fingerprints on the envelope fragments, or possibly they'll decipher the remnants of our address, or Mum's name. So yeah. I go with '*Gatsby*. Just to make life a little easier. Then when Mum hears there's another meeting tonight at Liss's she insists that I can't miss it, otherwise I'll fall behind on the reading homework, so I don't have to stay in tonight like Milly does. Milly throws an immediate strop and tells Mum she's going to bed without any tea.

ELLA

'So how come you decided not to go to Buzz Club tonight?' Maz says, turning my vibrator back on and scrolling the speed up. He touches it to his willy and shivers. 'That feels very weird.'

I crack a smile, because he's being super cute about the whole vibrator-joining-the-party thing.

'They're talking about kinks actually.'

'What? And you're missing out!'

'What am I missing? I'm the OG on that sort of stuff. I've had a mukbang and ASMR channel for years.'

'Are they kinks?'

I shrug. 'My content will be for some people. Just for some reason it's classed as mainstream and PG, and other things aren't so . . . out in the open. Whereas having one of these *if you're a teenage girl* . . . !' I turn the speed up on my vibrator again. 'It's just your usual double standards and mixed messages from society.'

My phone lights up on the bedside table. Mum will be home in twenty minutes.

'I dunno . . . The mukbang and ASMR thing's probably had its time,' I say. 'I might shut it down.'

'Yeah? What're you going to do next?'

'I had a couple of ideas . . . But Mum's messed me around on them.'

'Oh.' He pouts. 'I could help, if you want me to . . . ?'

Maz's furrowed forehead is just too cute for me to reject him immediately. So I nod and smile. 'Yeah, maybe you *can* help me . . .' I peck him on the lips, sit up and lean over to grab my phone. 'You fancy a chippy delivery from Glenn's and then a walk up to Dawson Park? I'm not in the mood to be here when Mum gets home.'

There's a girl sitting on the swings alone when we get to the park. I don't really want to bother her, but I also want to check she's okay first before we give her a wide berth.

'Oh! It's you,' I say when we're close. 'Maz, this is Tavi's wee sister.'

'Hi!' He waves and sits down on a bench to look at his phone. I don't give this boy enough credit. I know this is his way of giving us some privacy.

I notice Wee Sis checking our surrounds. Scanning for threats almost. 'You alright?' I say.

'Yeah, fine. Is Tavi with you?'

'Nope. Why?'

'No reason,' she says quickly, resuming her gum chewing.

'You here on your own?'

She doesn't reply and kicks her foot against the rubber ground.

'Not a talker? I can respect that.' I sit, and we swing

back and forth on our swings for a bit. 'Tavi's at Book Club tonight, isn't she?' I say to make conversation. I'm not sure why I'm interrupting my walk with Maz to chat to this kid. But there's something about Wee Sis's vibe that's keeping me here.

'Yeah!' she scoffs. 'Tavi's at *Book Club*! Tavi gets to do *whatever* she wants. I'm the one who has to stay in and do my homework!'

Unsympathetic to this sibling jealousy bollocks, I get up to leave, but then she adds something that makes me stop.

'She's such a narcissist! Axel's right.'

'Sorry? What?'

'Tavi's a narcissist!'

I sit back on the swing, frowning. I glance to Maz – he's engrossed with his phone. I can hear some sort of sports commentary and a referee whistle, a crowd cheering. I look back to Wee Sis. 'Who said Tavi's a narcissist?'

She shrugs, pausing her gum chewing briefly, to say, 'I did.'

'Did you now . . .'

Her attention drifts up the park.

I follow and see two people walking down the lamplit path from Arbroath Road. One of them I'd recognise a mile off.

'Maz!' I say, flicking my head in their direction when he looks up. 'Axel.'

Maz gets up and walks to meet them. I watch Axel, lip-read their *hellos*. See Maz gesture towards us here on the swings. Axel seems reluctant to look over, then finally just a glance. Two KFC boxes in his hand. And another box in the hand of the girl standing beside him.

'Who's that?' I say to Wee Sis.

'Axel Mikkelson.'

'No shit! The wee girl, I mean.'

'My mate Anusha. You literally met her at Tavi's birthday.'

'Oh yeah!' I say, squinting to try and get her face in focus. 'The one I have a video of, rubbing Tavi's vibrator all over her legs and face?'

'Eh . . . You have a video?'

I don't answer, and instead I watch the body language between Axel and this wee lass *Anusha*. Or more Anusha's body language, because Axel knows I'm watching him. And knows he shouldn't fucking be here, hanging out in the park with Tavi's little sister and her friend. Buying them KFC and acting like the big man.

And apparently filling Wee Sis's head with some shite that Tavi's a narcissist!

I'm done. No more softly-softly. No more playing.

It's time for the real revolution.

Time to stop the Axel Mikkelsons of this world from using and abusing a girl, then dumping her to move on to the younger model. No more gaslighting. Shutting us down. Ignoring us.

'Remind me – what's *your* name?' I say.

'Milly—!'

'Want to be part of a revolution, Milly?' I say, keeping my squinted-eyes trained on the others.

She says, 'What sort of revolution?'

I tap my nose. 'It's on a need-to-know basis. A secret. You're either in or out.'

'Does Tavi know about it?'

I look at her. 'Maybe. But only because *I* made her chairperson.' I sniff and stand. Look at one of my nails. It's bright Barbie pink: OPI's *Emflowered*. And now I know how I'm going to do this. 'You're probably too young,' I say.

Milly bites. 'I'm sixteen in a month! I can literally vote in Scottish elections. I'm legal to have sex. I can even get married!'

Can you get married at sixteen? Ugh! Why would you want to?

'You're maybe old enough. But Tavi probably wouldn't like it. Forget I said anything. Especially if you're hanging with Axel . . .'

Milly shakes her head frustrated. 'I'm not. Anusha is.'

I nod, seeing the situation clearer. But still hating Axel Mikkelson. 'Then do your friend a favour and take her home. It's dark. There are dodgy people about.'

'Axel's here. You're here.'

'You've seen Axel with your sister, Milly. You know better

than anyone, he's not someone little girls should hang about with.'

The others approach, getting within hearing distance, so I verbally sidestep. 'Axel! Fancy seeing you here. And with Tavi's wee sister's friend too. Funny that.' I walk over to him and take one of the KFC boxes and I hand it to Milly. 'Tavi was just messaging me, wondering if I'll pop over and get a book from Book Club. So I'll walk you girls home. Maz, I'll call you later about that *thing* you're helping me with!'

The wee friend pipes up, 'I'm staying—'

'Nah, love!' I say deadly. 'You're coming with me.'

TAVI

'Let's get kinky!' Eve says, flicking the feathers attached to the end of her pen in the air like it's a tickle wand – she's acting as club secretary and taking Buzz Club minutes in the femual. 'What's your vibe? Your buzz. Fetish. Kink. What've you got for me, ladies?'

Other than a grumble of embarrassment and awkward jokes, we all just look at each other.

'Come on! What do you think about when you're using your vibrator? Who. What. Where . . . Anyone? This is going to have to be your Buzz Club homework if you don't already know what turns you on.'

'I've got a shoe fetish!' Khair jokes.

'Yeah, but do you think about shoes when you're wanking?' George says.

'George!' Eve says. 'Do you have to use that word?'

'What, *wank*?'

Eve physically squirms.

'Ooh, I love a bit of *wanky panky*, don't you, guys?' George shimmies.

'Stop it!' Eve says.

'Eve, make sure you write wanky panky in the minutes!'

'Do I have to . . . ?'

'I've got one,' Ijeoma volunteers.

We all fall silent.

Larissa is the only one who moves, to flick her hair. A blonde lock falls onto my sleeve and I zone in on it for a moment until Ijeoma speaks.

'I've been listening to this vintage music to get me in the mood for *wanky panky*.' Ijeoma winks at George for inventing this phrase.

And it crosses my mind how much more relaxed Ijeoma seems to be, here in Liss's house than she was in Ella's. To be fair, I feel the same. Liss's house has a calm atmosphere.

'Like classical music?' someone asks.

'Ah!' one of the new girls yelps. 'It's *got* to be "The Ride of the Valkyries" – that crescendo at the end!'

I remember she sang solo in assembly the other week

– Felicity, that's her name. She finds us the song on her phone and – as she plays it full volume – the strings and wind instruments at the start give me this weird, swiping, teasing, build-up sensation in my body. Like auditory foreplay. We all seem to be feeling it as a couple of girls make a thing of flinching along as the music builds. Felicity suddenly cuts the music off, leaving us riled and quiet.

Eve breaks the tension. 'We should make an ultimate *play* list!' She winks. 'And we'll each contribute our favourite *good vibes* music!'

'Cute, Eve.'

'Do I have to pick only one?' Felicity moans. 'I have two favourites. Here . . .'

A fully ominous choir and orchestra booms from her phone. Tension building into kettle drums, and fanfares, and we're all subjected to what sounds like an angel of death, musical gangbang. Enduring it, I feel my entire body tighten and recoil in revulsion. It's like a deep-rooted reaction. A turning off. Until we get to the end of the explosive fireworks and drum-beating.

The music stops.

'I don't think I like that one . . .' I say uncomfortably.

Liss says beside me, 'It is quite masculine and aggressive. Perhaps the first piece of music would be less . . . triggering?'

I quickly look at Liss. Was Axel like that with her too?

She smiles at me. Like we share something. Like I'm not alone in how I feel.

'"Ride of the Valkyries" it is then,' Felicity says easily.

And George says, 'Talking about triggers . . . Remember that time the bomb squad blew up my vibrator!'

And as we descend into hysterics, I feel lighter again. I'm part of this club. We're having fun. We can make jokes about stuff and even if someone doesn't like something that's said, there are others to back them up. Or to call them out. This is a safe place.

Eventually we calm down enough that Ijeoma gets to tell us the *good vibes* music she'd actually meant – her contribution to the *play* list – and it really surprises me. I can see why Felicity suggested the dramatic music. But it just shows you can't judge people on appearances. Because Ijeoma plays the sweetest, summeriest, flower-filled meadow, pretty girl with long, flowing golden hair and butterflies flitting through the air . . . that you've ever heard embodied in a song. And as I listen to it, I find myself once again involved with the lock of Liss's hair resting on my upper arm.

'Wow . . . !' George says.

'That's beautiful,' Liss says.

Ijeoma smiles and says simply, 'Yes.'

'Okay!' Eve stretches. 'Anyone for bondage?'

* * *

'Is Milly in bed?' I ask Mum once we're home from Liss's house.

'Yep. She wouldn't have any dinner. See if she wants some toasted cheese or something for supper?'

'Okay . . .' I tramp up the stairs.

'Aren't you going to take your puffer jacket off?'

'Yeah. I will. Just keeping the warmth inside for a bit,' I lie. Up in my room I unzip my jacket and remove the femual and shove it under my bed. I put my phone on charge and go out onto the landing. And knock on Milly's door. When I don't get a reply I stick my head in anyway.

'What?' She's lying on her bed looking at her phone.

'You alright?'

'Yep. Have a nice time at *Book Club*?'

'Yeah. Mum wants to know if you want some toasted cheese.'

'I had a KFC.'

'Did you? How?'

'Got a delivery to the alleyway. Don't tell Mum.'

'Okay. Night then.'

Once I've heard Mum and Dad go to bed and I'm tucked up myself, with my door barricade in place, I allow myself to think about tonight's meeting. Two things in particular. The first was the big announcement from Liss and Ijeoma.

At least, I thought it was a big announcement but everyone else seemed to take it in their stride. They're seeing each other. Liss told us she'd been thinking about Ijeoma for months and that's who she's been thinking about when she uses her vibrator and then Ijeoma replied with this massive grin that she'd been picturing Liss when she listened to that music. And everyone screamed and clapped. And then Liss leant over and kissed Ijeoma. So everyone screamed louder and hugged them.

I realised on the way home why I was feeling confused emotionally about this news. It throws a whole bucketful of doubts on Axel's claims that Liss asked him out and that she's trying to break us up. And if that isn't true, then what else isn't?

And then there's that music and Liss's golden hair resting on my arm . . . And the way it's made me feel. It's made me want to use my birthday present. So much so, that I plug it in to charge it.

And the act of finally doing this only amplifies my confusion.

I thought I was straight. I thought I was into guys. Into Axel. So why doesn't thinking about Axel make me want to plug in my vibrator?

Why does thinking about Liss in some idyllic nineteen-seventies floaty movie have me excited?

CHAPTER 22

TAVI

'How was Book Club last night?' Axel says as soon as he sits beside me in the Upper Common Room before class.

'Uh, yeah. It was good . . . Thanks.'

Axel's silent for a while. I'm not sure how he knows I went. I wait for the explosion because I chose Book Club over *us*. Instead, he starts whistling to himself.

'How was your night?' I ask lightly.

'Boring. I stayed in again.'

Maz arrives, and slumps down on Axel's other side. 'Morning,' he grumbles.

'Where's Ella?' Axel says.

'*Running girly errands,*' Maz answers. 'She'll be in by first break.'

'So did Ella get that book from you?' Axel asks me in

this affected nonchalant way that makes me think he's up to something.

'What book?'

'I don't know . . .'

Maz says, 'She walked your sister home because she was collecting a book from you.'

'What do you mean, walked my sister home? Are you talking about two nights ago? When she was out in Dawson Park?'

Maz frowns and turns to look at me properly. '*Last night.* They were in Dawson Park.'

'Who's *they*?'

Maz looks to Axel.

Axel shrugs. 'I presumed you knew. I happened to pass them on their own and went and got them KFC because they said they were hungry.'

'Were you with them on Monday night too?'

'I'm not sure what you're insinuating!'

'Insinuating? I'm asking straight up whether you were hanging out in the park with my little sister on Monday— You literally just said you stayed in last night! Again! So were you lying?'

'I'm not listening to this if you're going to shout at me. You're acting mental!' Axel grabs his bag and he's off across the common room.

But I'm so fucking angry this time, I don't let him off

with his usual, so I follow and quickly push out through the swing doors into the hall.

I track him along the hallway and round into the Science corridor. 'What the fuck, Tavi—!' he says when I grab his school bag from behind and tug. 'You've lost it!'

'Have I though? Or am I finally seeing you for who you really are?'

'Let go of my bag. You're being totally aggressive. No wonder I went out to the park for a walk. I'm dealing with all this stress caused by you. You're literally abusing me!'

'*I'm* abusing *you*?'

'Yeah!' He points to his bag and tugs it weakly.

I let go. And feel my righteous fight drain away. I'm tired of all this.

'God! And you expect me to get turned on when you're like this?' Axel shrugs his blazer onto his shoulders and pulls his bag up straight. 'You need to take a bit of responsibility for your side of our relationship, Tavi. Behave with a bit of dignity!' His sneer makes me feel insane. Like I'm this vulgar nutter who just totally overreacted when all he was doing was getting Milly something for her tea and looking out for her, while I was off messing about with sex toys with all the girls.

Only . . . that's absolutely where I'd rather be right now. I don't *want* him.

I want to have fun. I want to spend time with my Buzz

Club friends. To feel relaxed, and safe, and, yes, turned on!

On my terms. Not his.

Not his aggression. Or physicality. Not his kink. Fetish.

Mine. Whatever my imagination conjures. Mine. Whoever I think of when I listen to Ijeoma's music. *Mine*. The soft rallying of the Valkyries, not the brutal smashing of that other song. That music was pure Axel. Liss heard it too. I'm sure she did. Liss, who was *never* after Axel. Never trying to break us up. I know it now. All lies from him, to keep me apart from her and Ella. To keep me his. And no one else's.

He's not mine.

Not anymore.

I'm not his.

'Where are you going?' Axel shouts after me. 'Tavi! Don't you walk away from us! It's over! I won't hang around for you—! Tavi!'

ELLA

'Thanks, Yaya! You're an absolute legend!'

'That I am, Eleanora! But you promise you won't get in trouble for them?'

'Course not! No one will know. They're so discreet.'

'Well, yes. As I said, in my day they weren't like that.'

'I'd better get inside now. I've got to prep for this lunchtime presentation with my new disciples.'

'Okay. I'll see you at home later. Here, don't forget your coffee.'

I give Yaya a kiss on the cheek and get out of the taxi. And walk into school with my LV weekender slung over my shoulder like I'm a main character in a film slo-moing into battle. I'm here, girlies. I may have been up all night editing and plotting, but now I'm ready for the lipstick revolution!

TAVI

I manage to get Milly alone just before lunch, to try and find out what's going on, but she's not having any of it.

'*You're* out with your friends all the time!' she snaps back at me. '*And* you've snuck out to see Axel loads! Why should I stay at home while you get to mess around with your book club?'

'It's different!'

'How?'

'You're younger.'

'You'd just turned sixteen when you started with Axel. We're not that far apart. I'm so sick of you treating me like I'm a toddler!'

'I'm *not* treating you like a toddler!'

'Anyway, what am I doing that's so bad? I literally went and hung out in the park with my friend and we got some food. And we happened to meet up with *your* boyfriend. You spend time with him on your own! Why can't we hang out with him? You were busy!'

'You don't get it! Axel's . . .'

'Axel's what? Friendly? Actually talks to me? Looks out for me, like he's my brother?'

'No. I'm trying to look out for you. *I'm* your sister . . .' She's making me question myself now.

Then she goes for my throat, saying, 'You want to be the centre of everything – that's why you're in charge of that book club, isn't it! And Axel and me are supposed to just wait around until you're ready to give us attention. Well, we're sick of it!'

'Oh, really? Maybe I'm sick of you and Axel!'

Milly looks at her watch and mutters, 'Narcissist,' under her breath. Then, 'Are you done? I need to be somewhere.'

'No. I'm not done! And quit throwing big words like *narcissist* around. You don't even know what it means!'

Milly shrugs. 'Maybe you'd rather I used a smaller word – bitch!'

'That's it. I'm telling Mum and Dad you sneaked out.'

'Oh, sneak off . . . snitch!' Milly flicks her hand at me and stomps off along the corridor.

I bite my bottom lip as helpless tears block her from my sight.

ELLA

I smile as two more Year Eleven girls slip into the back-row seats of the empty school theatre, ready for my presentation. 'Hello, ladies. Good to see you. Hello . . .' I've trained a spotlight onto my mark a couple of rows in front. So that I appear *relaxed* – leaning against the back of a seat – but very much at the centre of everything.

I wait a little longer and once we've hit a tally of seventeen girls from Year Eleven and Twelve, Milly – Tavi's wee sister – gives me the nod that everyone's in. I murmur into my head mic and say, 'Lock the doors please, Chelsea.' And my production minion locks the theatre doors to give us privacy.

I leave my mark in the spotlight and head up to the sound and lighting control room. Once I'm there, I dim the lights, flick on the projector and speak into my mic. 'Enjoy the movie, ladies. Afterwards, I'm available to answer any questions. Don't forget there's a Buzz Club goody bag to collect at the end, including your instructions and your own personal femual. Enjoy.'

The theatre curtains open to display the screen saver

for the short film I spent all night creating and editing. *BUZZ CLUB'S LIPSTICK REVOLUTION*. And then it starts, and my voice fills the auditorium as a montage of film footage and photography of women fighting for their rights accompanies my words.

'All around the world, women, girls, female and identifying, are losing autonomy of their own bodies. Laws are repealed. Politicians overrule medical professionals. Blobs of cells are prioritised over living, breathing, humans.'

I'll work on my delivery for next time – I sound newsreader-ish.

'We've muted our own voices – miming and montaging to sound bites and trending songs on social media. Filtered our real faces. Attached claws to our fingers. Inflated our lips, breasts, butts . . . We're living Barbie dolls. Products of mixed and subliminal messages, fed to us by adults.' My stern voice pauses to show a still-life arrangement of all the make-up that I showed Mum. The camera zooms close-up on the base of all the knocked-over lipsticks, varnishes and shadows. Showing their labels. Over and over, until the block-capital names appear stamped on the screen. Overlapping, more and more with all the ridiculous words that some rhyming-obsessed marketing freak thought it appropriate to stamp on the bottom of a *cruelty-free* lippy or gloss. Cruelty free? Sure.

* * *

When the movie finishes and I've partially raised the lights, I walk along to my initial mark and into the spotlight once more.

The girls closest to me shift in their budget, school theatre seats and blink bleary-eyed. They look like they've been bombarded. Good. We have! All our lives.

'I know that felt super deep,' I say, touchy feely, 'and maybe not even relevant to you. You're probably turned off by serious stuff because, yeah, you already know life can be shit for females, girls, however you identify, and no doubt you just want to have a bit of fun and look pretty. Or hot. Or sexy . . . Whatever you're trying to achieve. And why not? It's *your* body. Why shouldn't you do what you want with it, right?'

I get a nose scrunch of endorsement and a couple of nods.

'But then the adults always have an opinion on how we should behave, don't they. It's like that iconic speech in the Barbie movie. We're allowed to speak our minds, as long as we're kind. But what happens when *they're* not listening? What happens when they're gaslighting us? Talking over us. Why should we be kind then? Boys don't get told to be kind all the time. They get to be *decent*. *Considerate*. I can be considerate. If you're being considerate to me. I can even be considerate if you've just been a dick and ignored me and repeated back what I just said as if it was your unique idea. *Consider-ing* you're lacking in social niceties and not deserving of me showing you kindness . . .' I remember I'm supposed to be using the make-up analogies.

I pick up my script again. 'We're allowed to play with make-up, even when we're wee, but we shouldn't put on too much! We shouldn't look too old. Too mature. We can look pretty, but even as teens they'd rather we didn't look sexy!

'But there's no age limit on buying make-up, is there. Why should there be? The worst that can happen is, what? We get exposed to toxic chemicals. Or we get our hands on something with retinols and give ourselves vitamin A poisoning?

'So does someone want to tell me why they're labelling nail varnishes or lip-gloss colours names like – *My Very First Knockwurst* or *First Time* or *Unbroken?*'

'Euww!' someone says.

I make a face as if to say *exactly!* 'And you're not telling me those names are targeted at forty-year-old virgins!

'It's always the nails or the lips, isn't it! Always those products. Those body parts that *they* fetishise. Because they're not selling us a product to moisturise or brighten. No. They're selling us sex! But not sex from our point of view. Because as much as I appreciate that a girl with plump soft lips and glossy talons kissing you, or sucking you, or scratching you, might be some of your ideal Friday-night-in activities, it ain't all of ours! So who is that creepy branding for? And what is its aim?'

I see a girl retrieve her make-up bag and open it.

'Even if those names *are* targeted at adults,' I add, 'I don't want any of that dysfunctional, submissive, keep-quiet-and-do-what-you're-told, you're an orifice or receptacle shite . . .' I wave my hand and shiver with revulsion.

But then I see a couple of girls exchange the sort of look that the rest of Buzz Club usually make when I speak, and I realise I've gone off on a tangent again. This was why I prerecorded my voiceover so that I wouldn't go all dark and sordid when I'm supposed to be spreading the word of pleasure, free speech and owning our own orgasms.

'Anyway, my point. We aren't the ones who sexualised the make-up. They did that for us. So why shouldn't we go with their theme and have a bit of fun too? I'm not one to gatekeep the power in my hands.' I laugh, trying to drag the energy up. 'So that's why I'm following my dad's one and only piece of life advice: *"Don't sweat the big stuff."* We're going to start this revolution by concentrating on the smallest of things. With our voices. And a teeny-tiny lipstick vibrator . . .'

CHAPTER 23

LISS

It's nearing the end of lunch break and Ijeoma and I are outside, sitting against school's boundary wall.

I'm midway through typing a message to Ella when Ijeoma says, 'Do you really think Ella's capable of helping in a delicate situation like this . . . ?'

This stops me in my tracks. I watch Ijeoma run a braid between her thumb and forefinger before she finally flicks it away and elaborates, 'You have to admit, last night's Buzz Club without Ella was more relaxed than the previous Buzz Club meetings.'

'You think I shouldn't even tell Ella we're meeting . . . ?'

She shrugs. 'I actually don't know.' And bites the tip of her thumbnail, thinking. 'It does seem like an emergency. And you know Ella, and Tavi, better than me.'

Half an hour ago, Ijeoma and I found Tavi completely in bits, crying in the changing rooms.

Ranting incoherently: 'He twists it all. Then *I'm* the wrong one! Milly shouldn't be out with him. She and Anusha shouldn't be meeting up with him in secret. In the park! He's not nice, you know, Liss. He broke my necklace, it wasn't me. He broke it on purpose! But it's never his fault. You know what he's like . . . ?'

Had I not witnessed Axel blame Tavi for her broken Tiffany necklace yesterday most of what she said would've meant very little to me. Axel's always been decent with me. I know that doesn't translate that he's decent to Tavi or other people. But there are things he's said about Tavi that have shocked me. And things he's apparently told Tavi that I've said that seem insanely ludicrous. Nasty. And over the last couple of weeks, I've started to realise that Tavi seems entirely lovely. Not the person Axel's made her out to be at all. And there's her necklace. I clearly remember him saying Tavi was clumsy for breaking her necklace. And now, looking back, in the back of my memory I'm remembering times he blamed me for things he did. Little things. Insignificant. But still, not my fault.

'I should've told Tavi on Tuesday morning that I saw Axel with her little sister and friend beside the park gates,' Ijeoma says shaking her head. 'Not just asked cryptic questions about their age!'

'Yeah, well, at least Tavi knows now,' I say.

'He's dangerous, you know, Liss. He's not safe for them to hang around with.'

'Axel's not *dangerous* . . . !'

Ijeoma grimaces and says, 'I don't know. What Tavi was saying. It doesn't feel right.'

I sigh deeply. Because I don't know now either. 'We need Ella's input,' I say decisively. 'She'll know how to handle this. She knows Axel too.'

Ijeoma pouts, but nods. 'Fine. I'll defer to you on this . . .' And her face settles into this indulgent soft smile.

It makes me warm. 'What . . . ?' I finally say with an incongruous shiver, once I've finally sent Ella the message.

'Nothing. I'm just looking at you.'

'I know. You're making me feel . . .'

'What?'

'Like I wish we were at home.'

'What can we do at home that we can't do here, Liss?' Ijeoma says, all innocent.

I glance across the grass, back towards the main school building. 'I may have a few ideas . . .' I'm failing to hide my cheeky smirk.

'Oh yeah?'

'I don't suppose you'd like to come to mine again tonight, would you? Maybe we could talk through my *ideas*. Or I could show you?'

She laughs. 'Both sound fun! Or you chould come to my house?'

'Oh? Yes. I'd love that!' I feel this bright, open, excited sensation rush my entire body, making me want to shiver again.

'Great,' Ijeoma says brightly.

We remain still, beaming at each other. And this feeling of serene happiness settles between us. I reach out and carefully wind my fingers through hers. We lean together. And kiss.

ELLA

Liss Chat.

> **Liss:** We're having an emergency Book Club meeting straight after school. Tavi's a bit of a mess emotionally about Axel. I've managed to get a private study room under the guise of Book Club for 4.30pm. Please will you come?
> Liss xx

TAVI

'I don't think I can stay out another night,' I say stiffly to Liss when she suggests Book Club.

'Totally know what you mean. That's why we're thinking a Book Club social in one of the after-school club rooms. A few snacks at the end of classes. Ella's coming. You know what she's like if there's food involved.'

'Ella said she'll be there?' I could really do with some of Ella's fight energy right now.

'Yep!' Liss says, pulling the bobble from her hair, releasing her bun, and her long golden waves fall around her shoulders.

I blink. Feeling unexpectedly strange. Like I'm suddenly closer to the sun and its rays are licking every cell in my body.

And then Liss twists her hair and bundles it back up again. Secures it with the band.

And I feel better. I watch her pat the back to check for loose strands.

'So what do you think?' Liss finally says.

'Okay,' I say. 'I can probably stay for a bit.' I need to work out what's going on with me. I thought it was Liss I was thinking about this morning but maybe . . . Surely it's not her hair! Larissa Perfect Fucking Hair Ferucci?

Larissa's Perfect Fucking Hair . . . !

* * *

When I get to the study room, the Buzz Club social's already started.

'How did Olly take the official break-up, Eve?' Khair says.

'You've finally split!' George says. 'Thank God!'

Eve shakes her head. 'Didn't even touch him. Like he literally shrugged and said, "You've looked like a boy ever since you cut your hair anyway."'

'Dick!'

I focus on Eve's hair with renewed interest, mulling over how I feel about her short pixie style. I have to admit that I'm not into it. The last thing I want to do is identify with Olly Standish, because increasingly he sounds awful. But I found Eve's long hair so much more *alluring* . . . ? Not sure I've ever used that word before.

'It's fine,' Eve says. 'Since I got my vibe, I've realised how totally selfish he is in bed anyway. The next guy better be ready to learn about what *does it for me* otherwise he's not getting to touch any of this!' She gestures to her body and then leans forward across the table to grab another handful of crisps.

'Fair point,' Khair says. 'If I ever *do* get a boyfriend, he's going to have a lot to live up to. Did you know most girls can't orgasm with just penetrative sex!'

'Yeah, we learned that in Sex Ed,' George says. 'Most of us need clitoral stimulation too.'

Ella says, 'Just use the vibrator on your clit while you're having sex. Win-win.'

A number of girls snort and grunt.

'Yeah, that doesn't sound entirely terrible,' George admits.

'I'd rather just have the vibe, thank you very much,' one of the new girls says. 'I'd rather not have anyone else near me.'

'Solo play is very much endorsed. Whether you're Ace or not. I mean, as long as you're having fun,' Eve says. 'It should be fun, shouldn't it? Olly and I had okayish sex. But if it's the right guy – person – and they respect you, you still don't have to want sex. Especially now we have our vibrators. If we didn't want to have sex with anyone at all we could still have a good relationship.' Eve looks straight at me.

A number of the others squint, and I spot raised eyebrows.

'What are you on about?' George says.

'I think Eve means,' Liss says carefully, 'that it's okay to not want sex? You shouldn't have sex if you're not ready. You shouldn't be pressured into it just to stay with whoever you're dating. Same with your vibrator. You don't have to use it if you don't want to.' Now Liss seems to be speaking directly to me too.

Ella says, 'I *love* sex! And I *love* my vibrator.'

'I'm into sex!' I blurt.

Everyone stares at me.

I can feel myself puce. But I push on and clarify, 'Just not his type of sex.'

They're quiet for a moment. And then Felicity the music girl says, 'Do you mean sex with boys?'

'No. I mean. I don't know . . . I meant . . .' I'm suddenly confused further by the memory of how turned on I was looking at Liss's hair yesterday.

'What then?' someone says gently.

'We're here for you, Tavi,' Liss says. 'You know that, right? All of us!'

I sigh and hug myself defensively. Trying to dodge now-serious expressions surrounding me.

'He didn't force you, did he?' someone says.

'No . . . Not . . . It's not what you think.'

'Tavi, this is sounding serious.'

Ella says, 'I knew that little shit was manipulating her!' Turning to Liss. 'Didn't I tell you—!'

'Oh, Tavi!' Eve's beside me and puts her arms round me.

I feel like a fraud. 'He's not manipulated me,' I say weakly. 'He just doesn't find me attractive!'

Ella snorts.

Everyone glares at her.

'I'm not laughing!' Ella balks. 'I'm fucking raging. Tavi, you're smoking hot! Axel's just addicted to porn.'

Everyone mutters.

'I'm serious. You know that fucks them up.' She says it to everyone. 'Rewires their brains so they can't get turned on by normal girls.'

'Eh?' George starts on her phone. Googling. 'She's right. Watching too much porn when you're young rewires your brain. Shit!'

I blink and side-eye Liss. I need to hear the truth. 'He told me you asked him out the Monday after my birthday party. That you were trying to break us up.'

Ella jumps in. '*He* asked *Liss* out! She knocked him back. Then of course he rebounded straight back to you.' Ella shrugs. 'We should've— Wait! You told me he couldn't get it up. Is that true?'

Everyone's silent.

I look down at my hands. 'It's just me. He can get a hard-on if . . .'

'What?' Ella says impatiently.

'If he . . .'

'She doesn't have to tell us,' Liss says.

'This is why we started Buzz Club!'

'Tavi, do you mind telling us? What's said in Buzz Club stays in Buzz Club.'

George mutters, 'That's *The Hangover*, not *Fight Club*.'

Eve glares at George. 'Honestly, Tavi, you've got me worried again!'

I blurt, 'He had to slap me and call me a dirty whore, then he could get a hard-on . . .'

They all stare at me.

I shrug, blinking. 'He didn't hit me that hard . . . And when he put his hands on my throat . . . It's just. I didn't really like it . . . It's not my *thing*.'

They're all still staring at me. Liss seems frozen. Then Ella breaks the night-terror paralysis. 'That little shit—!' She grabs her phone up, stabs *call* and sticks it to her ear.

'Ella! Who are— Don't call Axel!'

'I'm going to slap him into next week!' she growls. Then almost immediately shouts, 'He just hung up on me—!'

They all fall silent and stony-faced.

I've killed the atmosphere.

Then someone says grimly, 'That boy's hung up on himself.'

'I've watched porn,' someone pipes up. 'Have I rewired my brain too? What if I can't have a proper relationship because of it?'

'Surely a little bit of porn is okay?' someone else says.

'What about our vibrators then? Are they desensitising us?'

'More likely sensitising. I feel like mine woke my fud up.'

'George!'

'That's my favourite Scottish word – fud!'

'More like yours nearly blew your fud up!'

'You were only supposed to blow the bloody doors off!' George says in a funny accent.

'Eh?'

'Never mind.'

Eve says gently, 'Do you think we could get back to speaking to Tavi?'

'Oh! Sorry, Tavi.'

'Sorry, that was totally inappropriate.'

'You must feel traumatised, Tavi!'

'Tell us what we can do to help?'

'I'm okay,' I say. 'I'm kind of numb to it. I mean . . . It's his manipulation and lying and gaslighting that's bothering me still. I can contextualise Axel's sexual preferences now. But, as Eve said, sex should be fun and consenting on both sides. And I identified ages ago that I wasn't having fun and didn't want to have sex like that. He just didn't want to listen to what I was telling him.'

'Yeah, why's it so easy to gaslight girls? Even the teachers do it!'

'Not just to us. At parents' evening Mr Elliot kept talking over Mum, wouldn't let her get a word in edgeways. Kept saying that if Dad was there then it would've been better to discuss the complexities of my Maths A-level shortcomings. Even called her a housewife twice!' exclaims Khair.

We all frown and scrunch our noses at how offensive Mr Elliot is, especially because of his horrible beard and halitosis coffee breath.

Then Khair drops the punchline. 'Mum worked as an actuary in insurance for ten years. She only looks bedraggled when she comes into school because she's on extended maternity leave and none of us are getting any sleep because of my demon-spawn baby brother. My accountant dad always goes to Mum for help with calculations.'

Eve croaks, 'Olly used to tell me, "Your mouth wasn't designed for talking, Eve."'

'What *was* it designed for then? Eating?' someone asks.

'Sucking and swallowing,' George says darkly. 'His head's loose a few wires, Eve. You're well shot of him.'

Eve nods at George, sharing something between friends, and then when she meets my eyes, I'm included too.

'Right!' Ella says. 'Order of priorities. First – how do we deal with Axel? Then, revolution.'

CHAPTER 24

TAVI

I'm walking back home after the Buzz Club social, feeling a combination of relief, deflation and, dare I say it, love and friendship. Like I could tell them anything and they'd take it in their stride. Make jokes and quips. But not at my expense. They've brought me out of the dark into the light. Where I'm no longer alone. My problem shared – feels like it's in my past. And my future is . . . *my future*.

Ella calls me.

I answer, 'Hi.'

She announces in my ear, 'I need to tell Maz!'

'No, you don't, Ella!' I say.

'Tavi, Axel told him you were frigid! Surely you want him to know the truth?'

'I don't care what the boys think of me.'

'I do!' she says. 'And you're definitely dumping him for good now. Yes?'

'Well, I actually sort of already did . . . This morning. I found out he'd been hanging out in the park with Milly when he'd said he'd stayed at home. I yelled at him, he gaslit me – per usual – so I just walked away and ignored him.'

'Fuck, *finally*! Yeah. That wasn't cool. I did warn her.'

'Milly?'

'Yup. She's pretty bright actually. Apparently it was her friend who kept pushing to go hang with him. *She's* a weird one, isn't she.'

'Anusha's weird?'

'The one who put on the mime show with your vibrator at your birthday. I'm not sure I'd trust her still . . .'

'No? When were you talking to Milly and Anusha?'

'Uh, I was just talking to them earlier today. Better go. Just wanted to check you're alright. And that you're absolutely, definitely – completely and utterly – dropkicking Axel. But you've already done it so – yay! And remember to bring in the femual tomorrow – I'll update it with this afternoon's minutes. Or do it yourself. I don't care.'

'I'll see how much time I've got—' I add, 'We're not putting what I just told you about Axel in it!'

'No. That's your business. Well, it's our business now,

to help sort him out but . . . It's up to you what we do. And, just putting this out into the air – I have a great therapist. She'll know someone. If you want to talk to somebody else— It's an option. See you tomorrow!'

Milly meets me as soon as I'm in the front door. She glances upwards and says under her breath, 'Axel was here.'

'Where? Not in my bedroom?' I take the stairs two at a time and push into my room. Sitting on my bedside table is a vase of red roses and propped up against them is a sealed envelope labelled: *Octavia*.

I immediately check the USB socket behind the table. My vibrator's charger is still plugged in but there's no vibrator there. I used my vibe for the first time in the middle of the night. I can't totally remember where I put it this morning. I scan around my bed, look under it. See the pink glitter femual. Grab it and chuck it on my duvet so I won't forget it. And open the bottom drawer of my bedside table, about to pull the whole thing out, to check whether I returned the vibrator to its case after I'd washed it, like I'd planned, when I realise that I'm not alone . . . I look round and Milly's standing in the doorway with huge, wide eyes.

She says, 'You have a femual!'

LISS

We've turned the corner onto Ijeoma's street and I can't quite believe that this is happening. We're about to walk together in through Ijeoma's heart shaped gates, up her path, into her house. And meet her dad. I can barely breathe.

Then she takes my breath away completely, by saying, 'How do you feel about holding hands?'

'When . . . ?'

'Now.'

I glance back over my shoulder to the main road, where the buses pass. Beyond that, down the hill, is *my* house. Mum and Dad won't be home from work. But we haven't had any conversations yet. I did tell my brother, Jamie, last night. But he was so relaxed about it I may as well have told him I'd just found a missing sock. He offered to sit with me when I *do* decide to speak to our parents. But I need more time to think that over.

'No pressure,' Ijeoma says. 'It was just in case you wanted to. *Zero* pressure.'

We're almost at her gates. It would literally be for ten, twenty steps? But I don't feel ready for that. West Ferry is a small, gossipy place. I need to speak to Mum and Dad first. It's different with the Buzz Club girls. Freer.

'Your dad doesn't mind about stuff like that, does he?' I ask rather than say no.

She laughs but it's in a nice way. 'He'd be delighted. My parents are *big* on affection. Dad will probably ask if he can hug you hello.' She stops and looks concerned. 'I can ask him not to ask for a hug. I've got a couple of friends in my neurodiverse non-hetero group who won't be touched at all. Mum and Dad overcompensate by offering them extra snacks instead of hugs . . .'

I laugh. 'Snacks. Hugs. Either.'

Ijeoma doesn't push the hand holding anymore and we walk through the gates, then she's unlocking the front door, and I'm standing on the step with my heart in my mouth. 'Dad?' she calls from the porch. I feel so nervous.

But there's no answer. We find a note on the kitchen counter.

Just dropping off Mum's tea at the hospital. There are smoothies and flapjacks for after school snacks. Should be back by 6pm.

Hi, Liss! Welcome!
Dad xx

I sit on a bar stool while Ijeoma gets our snacks. 'Have you told your parents that we're actually . . . ?'

She sets the blender jug down full of a purple-pink smoothie. And finishes my sentence, 'a couple?'

I feel a blush of pleasure. 'Are we?'

'I think so,' she says sliding a flapjack on a side plate in front of me. 'What do you think?'

I scrunch my nose feeling my stomach bounce. 'I think so too.'

She grins. 'I told my parents that I thought we were. But don't worry. They know you haven't shared who you are with everyone yet. They won't say anything to anyone. This is a safe space for you.'

We're lying beside each other on Ijeoma's bed, kissing, when Ijeoma stops and says, 'You never experienced anything like that with Axel, did you?'

I shake my head. 'Nothing physically abusive. But . . .' I purse my lips and rock my head. 'He could be overbearing.'

'In what way?'

'You know I'm quite go-with-the-flow. But it would've been nice to be consulted or asked where I wanted to go, rather than told. Stuff like that.'

'That sounds like the way Ella treats you.'

Ijeoma's tone bruises me a little. But I just say, 'It looks like that on the surface, perhaps.' I shrug. 'I put boundaries up over the last couple of years, so no one could really hurt me. *Now* I'm letting them down.'

Ijeoma's forehead creases. 'Noted.'

'I spoke with Ella about you and me, yesterday.'

'Did you?' Ijeoma seems surprised.

'She says she's ready to *champion* us.'

'Ella Konstantinou championing me? Wow! Who needs enemies . . .' Ijeoma at least smiles, but she doesn't retract the bitchy comment.

I raise my eyebrows. If there's one thing I've learned, it's that I'm not going to change who I am or who my friends are, for anyone. No matter how much I might like them. Ella's my best mate. And that's that. I finally say as firm as I can without sounding like I'm being emotional, 'I respect that you don't like Ella very much. That many people find her loud and brash. But I *do* need *you* to respect that she's my friend. I don't have an interest in hearing people be nasty about her. Just as much as I wouldn't let someone speak badly about you in that way.'

Ijeoma's still, while she processes my words. And then I feel her relax against my side. 'Okay,' she says simply.

I smile.

'Now!' she says brightly. 'You were going to tell me about those ideas you had on what we *can* do here that we shouldn't at school . . .'

'I was, wasn't I . . .' I twist round further and tuck my hand under my cheek.

Ijeoma does the same so that our noses are almost

touching. I can still smell the hint of mint on her breath from her chewing gum earlier.

I say, 'I don't want to use our vibrators together.'

'Oh. Okay. Never?'

'Not the ones that Ella and I bought anyway. If we're going to buy some to use together, I'd like us to choose them *together*.'

She smiles and kisses my nose. 'That'll be fun!'

'Good. So, yeah. You know how we were talking about kinks in Buzz Club . . . ?'

Ijeoma's eyes light up. 'Now you're talking!'

I laugh, but I have to close my eyes and roll onto my back, because I'm too embarrassed to say what I want.

Ijeoma's having none of it. 'Come on!' She wraps her arms and legs round me in a full body hug and demands in my ear, 'Tell me now! If you tell me yours, I promise I'll tell you mine!'

She's being so silly I don't feel quite so embarrassed. I lock her in place with my own hug so that I at least don't have to look her in the eye, and say to her ear, 'How do you feel about feet?'

'Really?' Ijeoma struggles apart and looks at me properly.

'I've been obsessed with your feet, ever since we were at the eagle-wing sculpture when you got cramp.' I shrug. 'Obviously that's not the only part of you I'm into. But it's where I'd like to start.'

Ijeoma says, 'As long as you don't tie me up and tickle them with a feather, then I'm game.'

'Damn!' I say grinning. 'That's the first thing I have on my list.'

TAVI

Milly and I sit talking late. She tells me Ella's started a new Buzz Club revolution, to include the years below, but won't tell me how that differs to ours. I decide to have a word with Ella about this. I'm not telling Milly what she can and can't do. We're different – I've always been the overanxious sister and Milly's the confident one. But Milly's still naive. I need Ella's reassurance that she's not going to get her in trouble with school and our parents. All Milly will say is, *Don't worry, it's in my make-up bag!*

She apologises for sneaking about with Axel. And admits that Anusha has a massive crush on him. I admit that I'd noticed that. And ask after Anusha, hinting I'm worried about her sneaking about with *older* guys. I try to keep my concerns vague so I don't freak Milly out. But she tells me that Anusha's set her mind on a boy in their Biology class as of this afternoon, because – apparently – Axel's too *angry*.

I should laugh, but the fact Anusha has the sense and judgement to give Axel a wide berth, and I haven't – it's kind of depressing.

I tell Milly I've broken it off with Axel for good. Milly says she's glad, because the way Axel speaks to me sometimes has her wanting to rabbit punch him. This does make me laugh.

Then Milly tells me Ella said something last night that made her question everything she thought she knew about Axel. She doesn't elaborate. And I don't press her because I don't want to tell her the details of how Axel and I have been in private. I don't think she's ready for that. But this amplifies my regret that I've not been brave enough to call it with Axel before now. Milly isn't stupid but she also isn't untouched by my relationship with Axel. If she's noticed the way he's talked down to me, gaslit me . . . other stuff . . . how will that affect her relationships in the future? I don't want her to accept any of that. I decide to let her read Axel's letter.

Princess!
I've been thinking about you ever since we argued earlier and just had to write this letter to tell you how amazing, clever, caring, pretty and sexy you are. And how lucky I was to have you in my life. And now I've lost you!

I always knew I wasn't good enough for you, Tavi! You're probably relieved you don't have to put up with me anymore.

Bet there are loads of blokes in your DMs wanting to take my place. That makes me sick in my stomach. I want to fight them all. Tell them you're too good for them too!

But I know I don't have that right anymore. You trusted me and I chucked it back in your face. And for that I'm really sorry. I'm sorry I lied about going out to the park this week. I was hurting because you didn't want me and instead you were off with all the girls. Hanging out with my ex. When I'd told you she was trying to break us up. She's succeeded, hasn't she. And I can't quite believe it.

I know you're not confident when you're around Larissa. How she makes you feel ugly in comparison. But remember, I broke up with Larissa . . . I pursued you! That must show you how much I care about you, Tavi. How special you are!

Yeah, I know I fucked up and you don't want me anymore. But I'm making you a promise — I'll fix this! I'll prove I'm a good guy if it's the last thing I do. Even if it's too late for us as a couple. We can be friends. Can't we? Because I need you in my life, Tavi. I can't live without you. You get me. You and your family, even Douglas. I love them. And they love me. They do, don't they?

I was just trying to be a big brother to Milly. Looking out for her when she was out in the dark. Making sure she was safe. Got some food.

That's what David and Caroline want me to do, isn't it? Look after their girls.

David especially. I know you wouldn't tell him everything that's happened between us — that would be kinda sick — but please at least don't make things awkward between us, Tavi. You know your family's helped me work through things . . . And David and me have been like father and son, until now so please don't spoil that for me, Tavi. I don't know what I'll do if I can't spend time with you and your family.

And . . . This'll seem insignificant to you, but it would really affect me, more than you realise, if you went out with Standish. That would break me. Neil and Maz are off limits too, obviously. In fact, anyone from school! I couldn't live seeing you with someone else at school. You were telling me the truth about that lube, weren't you? You haven't been with anyone else? Have you? Doesn't really matter anymore anyway. So tell me the truth.

Anyways, I'm probably the last person you want

> to hear from tonight. I just wanted to give you these roses. They're beautiful and classy. Just like you!
>
> Always here for you,
> Axel xxx

'Ugh—!' Milly says once she's read it. 'That letter's *pure* emotional blackmail. Ignore him!'

'You think so too? I wasn't sure if I was being narcissistic, again.'

'Narcissistic . . . ? Oh! I was just saying that to wind you up. Axel called you it when we were chatting and—' She stops talking and screws her face up, incredulous. 'Shiiit . . . ! He's *so* manipulative, Tavi! He told me you were a narcissist because you *went out to Book Club and didn't care about spending time with him or me.* I was just repeating what he said. I'm really sorry.'

'That's okay. He *is* good at manipulating people.'

Milly quirks her head and looks at me seriously. Then she says, 'I know I'm your *little* sister. But I know enough to know that your relationship with Axel wasn't about love. You know that too, right?'

I can't bring myself to nod. I end up twitching a sort of sideways flick.

'Tavi. Even I could see that you and Axel have been . . . messy.'

That word triggers me. All I can think of is Axel telling me that Liss called me messy.

Milly's waiting for me to say something and instead my eyes end up glassing up with tears.

'Tavi?'

'Sorry.' I wipe my nose with the heel of my hand. 'I'm still trying to process . . . I don't know what I'm processing.'

'That you're better than Axel? That Axel's a massive *see you next Thursday?*'

'Mills!'

She quirks a smile. And flicks her eyebrows. 'He is though, isn't he! The way he keeps combing his hair with his fingers and always looks in that mirror in the kitchen. And talks over us when Dad's here.'

I scrunch up my nose in disgust and add, 'And his long nails on his right hand for plucking his guitar!' I shiver with revulsion.

'Bleugh!'

'They're so jabby!'

Mills shakes her head. 'Too much information.'

'Sorry.'

We sit in silence for a moment. And I feel a further release of tension. Like there was more to let go of, more than I'd acknowledged or realised during Buzz Club.

Then Milly says, 'I'm reading your book, by the way. You realise it describes Axel to a T . . .'

'What book?'

She slides off my bed and goes through to her room, returning with the copy of *Disarming the Narcissist* Ella gave me.

I grimace and let out a long sigh. Ella was trying to tell me what I should have spotted ages ago: Axel's the narcissist, not me.

I'm not sure whether I'm extra frustrated with myself that I let him mess with me for this long or whether I'm just relieved that everything's out in the open. And now that I've broken it off – he can't manipulate me, or Milly, again.

'Hey?' Milly says. 'Fancy coming with me to take Douglas for his late walk?'

'Sure.'

'Great. That means you can tell me the story about the lube.'

I laugh, and as I push my feet back into my shoes I say, 'Wait until you hear the story about how Douglas got into Mrs Stanton's conservatory. Or the one about the bomb squad and the bin!'

Milly gapes. 'Whhaaaaaaat . . . ? You need to start with that one!' She pulls open my bedroom door to let me out.

'Oh, wait! I'll just grab Axel's letter . . .'

'You're not showing Mum and Dad, are you?'

'Nope!' I say brightly, and practically skip along the landing.

'What are you going to do with it then?' Milly says, following.

'Use it to pick up Douglas's bedtime jobbie!'

CHAPTER 25

ELLA

I answer Maz's call as I'm walking in through the school gates. 'Hey! Sorry! I had to sort through the ingredients for our dinner tonight, with Yaya. I'm walking in now—'

'I'm coming to meet you then.'

'Okay. What's up? You sound serious.'

'Yeah. Uh, Axel knows! *All* the boys in the Upper Common Room know about Buzz Club. I'm not sure this is the best day for your Lipstick Revolution . . .'

I'm on the phone to Milly by the time Maz gets to me. I put her on speakerphone so he can hear. And reply to her garbling, 'I knew that friend of yours would be problematic. Have you spoken to your sister yet?'

'I *just* said bye to Tavi – she's heading to the common room. Then I came to form class!'

I exchange a look with Maz. I'm tempted to send him to the common room, but I don't yet. 'Tell me exactly what Anusha said.'

'She literally told me yesterday she wasn't into Axel anymore because he's too angry.'

I say grimly, 'She's got that right!'

'Yeah, well, I don't know if they planned it or if it was random, but they met this morning at the back of the sports pavilion and Nush was probably trying to act all mature and said she knew something he didn't about Tavi's book club, and then she just told him that it was a *secret vibrator club* and that she thought it was *totally desperate and pathetic*.'

'And today's just started. Where's Anusha now?'

'Like, two desks away. I walked away when I saw you were calling.'

'Right.' My head's whirring. 'Do you think she told Axel about the Lipstick Revolution?'

There's a pause. 'I don't think so. I can double-check. Do you still want us to go ahead with today's plan if Nush hasn't told him about it?'

'That's what I'm trying to work out.' I look to Maz and take Milly off speakerphone.

He nods, gives me a reassuring smile and sits down on

the floor across the corridor to wait. And I'm struck once again, at my luck for his steady support. He's always patiently waiting to find out what I want to do next. He came here immediately. Didn't side with Axel. Or the other boys. In what I can only guess is a sort of righteous, disgusted, wronged, holier-than-thou misogynistic war in the common room.

My head clears some, and I instruct Milly, 'Tell Anusha I'm going to show Axel that video of her at Tavi's birthday, rubbing the vibrator all over her legs, crotch and face if she tells anyone *anything* more about Buzz Club. I'll make sure he thinks *she's* been in the club from the start.'

'Got it.'

'And get her goody bag off her. I don't want her showing anyone what's in it. Even if she's used the lipstick! Get it off her.'

'Done.'

'And . . .' I pause, trying to visualise how this might play out. If seniors know about the existence of Buzz Club, how does that change the impact of our plan? Surely the news of this secret vibrator club will drip down (strategic choice of words) to the younger years. 'I think we still go ahead . . .' I say, staring into space.

'Do you want us to follow the original plan exactly . . . ?'

'Yes,' I say decisively. 'Stealth mode. Not a word. Let the *plan* do the talking.' I hang up.

'You okay?' Maz asks.

I walk to him and slide down the wall to snuggle under his arm. 'Mum's going to kill me when this kicks off.'

'No, she won't. She'll be proud of how clever you are. Me and your gran will make sure of it.'

TAVI

Ella takes all of Buzz Club out to La Luna for pizza over lunchtime so we can avoid the inevitable carnage planned by a certain collective of outraged boys. She's been strangely calm all day. Despite the volcanic rumblings.

This morning when I arrived in the Upper Common Room. I heard the words *Slapper*, *Hoor*, *Dildo*, buzzing sounds like bees . . . It took me moments to follow this tenor choir of voices back to the master at the centre, where Axel sat unbothered. Staring at his phone. His noise-cancelling headphones over his ears as if he had no idea, couldn't hear, what everyone else was volleying around the room.

It quickly became apparent, from the way some of the boys around him were reacting to his phone screen, that he was watching porn.

As the boys continued with their overconfident puerile insults, George was the first to match them. Volleying back with *porn addict!* And then all of Buzz Club started free-flowing insults. *Taker not a Giver. Dud Stud. Wham Bam No Thank You, Man. Slamateur.*

Axel's lackeys started muttering to themselves, before finally falling silent, not wanting to be targeted and singled out. And as they slunk out of range, leaving the common room, to protect their egos, they left Axel. Still intentionally oblivious with his headphones, sat alone staring at his porn.

ELLA

Milly reports in at the end of lunch to say that things are going as planned: in each class the girls started their *silent* protest – any time the boys or a teacher gaslit them, or talked over them.

She's handed out eight more of the new lipsticks I delivered this morning. They're going for phase two, *creating a buzz*, after lunch.

When we're walking back to school after pizza, I see that Liss is holding Ijeoma's hand. 'Liss, can I chat to you?' I say abruptly.

'Yeah?'

'Alone?'

Liss looks to Ijeoma, and says, 'Does it need to be in private . . . ?'

'Yeah. I wouldn't mind chatting to my best mate *in private*. If that's okay with you?'

Ijeoma puts her hands up as if to say she's not stopping me from speaking to Liss.

'Why are you being so rude?' Liss hisses. 'Ijeoma, sorry, do you mind if I do have a quick word with Ella?'

'I'm not being rude,' I say as Ijeoma falls back, giving us some privacy. 'I've got a lot on today and I just wanted to speak to you now while I've got time.'

'You *are* being rude and I've had enough of it. What do you want to speak about?'

'Well, I *was* going to say I haven't said anything to Maz about your private business . . .'

'Right.'

'And *you* won't tell Ijeoma my business either, will you?'

She doesn't reply and I'm starting to think she's already told Ijeoma about all my hang-ups. About me not knowing my dad. How I'll never be enough to live up to Mum's fame. How I know the girls here don't like me. And wish I'd shut up and go away. I guess girl code gets warped when we're all girls! Then she says, 'I'll never tell anyone your private business, Ella. You know I'm not like that. But, also, I know you respect my personal boundaries too.'

'Well, yeah. I do. Of course. I just had to check.' I shrug, not wanting to admit that I feel totally threatened by Ijeoma. Like I know Liss will end up hating me as much as Ijeoma does. She'll dump me as her friend. Tavi did the same when she started going out with Axel. But this time it'll be because my mate is in a *functional* relationship with healthy boundaries instead of a *dysfunctional* relationship where my friend got abused. 'Liss . . .' I say, checking the others aren't going to overhear me.

'What?'

'I just . . . I know you've never wanted to be chairperson of Buzz Club. And especially now it's all kicked off. But . . . you would have made a great chairperson. You'd be fair. You were the one who brought everyone together. You're the one with all the different people who like you and look up to you. All these different friends.' I point to everyone in our group. 'That's testament to you and what a good person you are.'

She's staring at me, eyebrows sky high, trying to suppress a smile, badly.

'What?' I say.

'Nothing, Ella. Absolutely nothing.'

TAVI

'Tavi!'

Axel appears from nowhere in the busy corridor when I'm waiting for Modern Studies class.

I don't say anything. I just take a step back, hugging my school bag to my side like it's protection.

'What the *fuck* is going on?' he says. 'Vibrators!'

I blink, but still I don't speak.

'Was it all a lie? You saying you didn't want to have sex. You didn't *like* it!' He doesn't even lower his voice. Acting blind to everyone walking past us. 'You *were* fucking around, weren't you. That lube! I knew it. Was it Standish? And you blamed Milly! That's sick, Tavi, even for you.'

He's too close to me now, cutting me off from the world. I stare just past his hip, at the blur of bodies passing us.

'What would David and Caroline say? You wouldn't be their little princess anymore if they knew what you've been doing!'

I shrink away and hit my back against the corridor wall.

He pushes against me and speaks low. 'Maybe I'll tell them. Shall I tell them, Tavi? Hmm? David'll be disgusted with you. You're disgusting, you know. Dirty little slut.'

I look up at Axel and narrow my eyes. 'Why would you do that?' I say. 'Why would you tell my parents?'

I see this expression of confusion wash over him. He shrugs as if to say, *I dunno. Because I can!*

I wrinkle my nose.

And suddenly an arm rams between us. 'Back the fuck up!' Ella says. 'Touch her again and I'll fucking batter you myself.'

Axel recoils. 'Maz, mate!' He puts his hands up, all light as a feather like he couldn't hurt a fly. 'Control your bampot.'

Maz is standing behind Ella. Just staring at Axel, red faced.

I look back to Axel. Does he see the change?

'You coming?' Axel says. 'None of us lads want to be seen around these sluts.'

I'm used to Axel speaking to me like this – he's an old vinyl stuck on repeat.

Ella's not.

And Maz certainly isn't used to hearing Axel speak about the girl he worships like that. I guess Axel forgot where he was for a moment. Who he was speaking to.

He's unlikely to forget it again.

Because Maz simply says, 'Sorry, *mate*, I'm not into that degrading, misogynistic, control shite you're into. And I hear Tavi feels the same. Probably time to shut up and listen.'

And without a pause, Ella punches Axel in the belly.

CHAPTER 26

TAVI

'Tavi! Is that you?' Mum shouts through as soon as I'm in the front door.

'Yeah! Milly was just finishing up on something! She's on her way.'

'Come in here!'

I dump my coat and bag, take my shoes off and pad to the family room. 'What's up?' I say. But as soon as I'm through the doorway I can see exactly what's up.

Mum and Dad are sitting on the sofa and in between them is my vibrator's neoprene case. *Open.* My vibrator's there, washed and tucked inside neatly, thank God – because I used it this morning.

Beside the vibrator are the packets of *GLIDE* lube that came with it. And in Mum's lap . . . the pink glitter femual. I'm immediately relieved that I didn't put anything about

Axel and me in there. But also, totally regretting not taking it straight to Ella this morning.

'Sit down,' Mum says.

I choose the armchair opposite them and tuck my stockinged feet up under me.

'What have you got to say for yourself?' Mum says. Dad's understandably mute. I can't even look at him.

I purse my lips and shrug.

'Axel tells us you're the leader of this *club*!' Mum waves the femual.

Axel? AXEL! What a fucking—

'I'm home!' Milly shouts through from the hall. 'Don't have a wobbler. I'm literally minutes later than Tavi!'

I decide to focus on the doorway rather than look at Mum, and definitely not Dad. That way I can see Milly's expression when she clocks the situation. And also, it gives me a breather from not breathing a word.

'Is there anything to eat . . .' Milly's words fade as she sizes the parentals in one glance, then her eyes fan the room and lock on me. We have a moment of connected telepathy. At least, I hope she's suddenly become telepathic because I'm shouting silently, *Don't say a word! I don't think they know about you!*

I say precisely, '*Axel* told Mum and Dad that I'm in a secret vibrator club. You know my book club? Well, *really* we've been talking about relationship issues and owning our own bodies and vibrators . . .'

Milly acts surprised, pouts and nods. 'Sweet! Can I join?' She walks towards the kitchen area.

'Tavi! Milly!' Mum says, cranking round to try and glare at Milly despite her now being safely behind Mum and Dad's sofa.

'What?' Milly says, leaning on the kitchen island. 'Sounds like a great set-up. Was I supposed to be outraged or disgusted or something?'

Mum glares back at me. She picks up a packet of GLIDE. 'These *were* yours then. You pretended you didn't know where they came from.'

I'm distracted by Milly walking back out past us again. 'Just need to grab something from my school bag,' she tosses over her shoulder.

'Tavi!' Mum says.

'Eh, yeah. I got those with the . . .' I murmur the last bit, 'vibrator. I hadn't realised they were mine until I saw them,' Milly comes back through, 'in the case.'

Milly dumps her bag on the kitchen island and rifles through it, and says matter-of-factly, 'You've seen Tavi's vibrator before, you know. That's the present Ella and Liss gave her on her birthday. Everyone saw it. Remember Anusha miming *bzzzzzz*!'

As Mum and Dad both rotate round to stare at Milly,

I take a moment to have an out-of-body experience and not laugh. Who knew my little sister was such a wise-cracking badass! Well, I did, actually. I just forgot.

She ignores them and takes out a lippy, removes the lid and runs it along her lip, frowns and looks at the bottom of the lipstick.

Mum and Dad turn back to me, but before either of them can say anything, an incredibly angry bumblebee sound starts behind them. And then I *realise*.

Milly's standing behind the kitchen island with a vibrating lipstick to her lips, casually reading her very own glittery pink femual.

'What's that noise . . . ?'
'What the hell!'
'That better not be—!'
'What's that book?'
'Has she got one too?'

All the while, my parents are getting louder and louder because Milly's pretending not to hear them over the buzz.

Turns out that's what the Buzz Club Lipstick Revolution has been doing all day. Pre-lunch, any time someone cut them off, spoke over them or ignored them, they immediately took out their lipsticks and acted unbothered. They daydreamed and stared into space as the person who interrupted them spoke or hogged the attention. All the while running their mini lipstick vibrator silently over their lips. All very meek and normal.

Then, after lunch, they turned things up a notch. Every time someone cut them off, gaslit them, spoke over them or simply didn't listen to what they had to say – they turned on their lipsticks and vibed to their own sound. And depending on how many of the Lipstick Revolution were in each class, that gaslighting, attention-hogging voice was either partially muted or entirely drowned out by the girls' buzzing.

It took longer for the teachers to realise what the lipsticks were than it took my parents. But by the end of the day the buzz around school was *all* about Buzz Club.

'Right. I'm off to bed,' I say after dinner.

'Me too,' Milly says.

'So early?' Mum says.

Milly says deadpan, 'Buzzy day ahead, Mum,' while packing her school bag. I see a flash of pink glitter inside.

So I think, *sod it*. Why shouldn't I be loud and proud about this? In my own home. I've got nothing to be ashamed of.

'What are you doing, Tavi?' Mum says.

'I'm taking this upstairs.' I zip closed my vibrator's

neoprene case. It's been sitting on the sideboard since we had our showdown earlier.

Mum says, 'You're not using that!'

'Eh, yeah, I am. Took me long enough to realise that this medical-grade silicone is the least toxic relationship in my life.'

'Excuse me?'

'I didn't mean you, Mum,' I say. 'That and I'm into long hair.'

Mum squints.

'It's my thing. Turns me on. So, yeah. I'm off to look at male models with long hair on the Internet.' I tap the case to my temple as if I'm saluting her *good night*. And I walk out of the family room to head upstairs with my vibe.

BUZZ CLUB's RULES REVISED

~~The First Rule of Buzz Club – *Do not talk about Buzz Club.*~~

The First Rule of Buzz Club – **Talk openly. And if they don't listen – buzz.**

Acknowledgements

Thanks for being brave, bold and loud along with me. And when I needed it – showing me kindness, consideration, patience and understanding.

I started the Buzz Club revolution, now it's your turn to be loud and proud.

Go create your buzz!

OUT NOW

A fresh, fierce and funny story about what happens when life literally goes to sh!t.

'FUNNY, DIRECT . . . AND ROMANTIC'
Guardian

'COMPELLING AND INSIGHTFUL'
Glamour

'WHIP-SMART'
Irish Independent